St. John
of the
Midfield

ISBN: 1-4196-7879-5

ISBN-13: 9781419678790

Visit www.booksurge.com to order additional copies.

St. John
of the
Midfield

Garasamo Maccagnone

TABLE OF CONTENTS

AUTHOR'S NOTE

THE ENCLOSED WRITINGS contain adult-oriented material. The content is not suitable for children or adolescents.

This story is based on actual events. All characters and scenes have been created through the author's imagination. Any similarity between the characters and real people are purely coincidental. The stories enclosed are purely fiction and relate to no person, no group, nor any organization.

If you would like to contact the author, go to his website at: **www.garasamomaccagnone.com**

To purchase books written by Garasamo Maccagnone, go to: **www.amazon.com**

DEDICATION

To: Coach Mike Jolly and all the other good coaches around our country who tirelessly work to keep kids in the game.

And to: All the parents of youth soccer players aspiring to be St. John of the Midfield. Teach them to... Honor the game. Respect their opponent. Chase Big Dreams.

Special thanks to: Maggie Cooper, Paula Lewis, Carla Stevens, Teri Carroll

FOREWORD

Maggie Cooper

ST. JOHN OF THE MIDFIELD is an easy reading, yet powerful story about personal courage in moments of adversity and devotion to the great game of soccer. Garasamo Maccagnone weaves an almost mystical story about Georgi "Bobo" Stoikov, a Bulgarian refugee who, after reaching America, finds work as a coach for a youth club travel soccer team.

A former world class soccer player in his native Bulgaria, Bobo has a magical way of inspiring his young American team members to go beyond their limits and win the State Cup Championship. Success, though, has a price and that price is quite high, not only for Bobo, but also for Luca, the most talented member of the team, who holds Bobo in high esteem.

Luca's father, Mario Santini, tells the story in which he is torn between hostility and admiration for his father—Grandpa Frankie—and the other Sicilian men in the family who belong to the Mafia. Mario, who feels trapped between his legitimate world and his father's illegitimate life style, is severely tempted to join his father's dark world when circumstances between him and an old nemesis of Bobo—the equally dark and sinister Sonny Christopher—reaches a boiling point.

Even if you are not soccer fan and don't know much about the Sicilian way of life, ST. JOHN OF THE MIDFIELD is still a book that will appeal to you. Its powerful emotional impact will keep you turning pages to the very end. The character Bobo Stoikov will stay in your heart for a long, long, time.

CHAPTER 1

I T DIDN'T MATTER that he was one of the greatest
soccer midfielders in the world. If he wanted to
live in America, Georgi "Bobo" Stoikov and his
older brother Jordan had less than fifteen seconds to
decide if they were going to jump off the train or be
arrested and returned to the Bulgarian city of Stara
Zagora to be tried as "enemies of the State."

"Go, Go, Go!" Jordan screamed, pushing Bobo out
of his seat toward the door. Bobo almost tripped down
the aisle as the train rocked. A guard shouted for them
to stop or he would shoot. Bobo and Jordan ignored his
warning. They ran like Olympic sprinters through the
car, through the open door, and were airborne before
the guard could raise his pistol.

There is no training in soccer which prepares anyone
to jump off a train moving sixty miles per hour. As
Bobo and I sat in Mancini's, one of suburban Detroit's
better Italian restaurants, he told me about his escape

to freedom, and said it looked easy in the bootlegged American westerns he had watched as a kid.

"You supposed to tuck and roll," he said, in his thick gravelly Bulgarian accent. "I only tuck."

It had cost him dearly. When Bobo hit the icy snow, he skidded like a motorcyclist on to a freeway after being tossed from the seat of his bike. Bobo's back hit hidden rocks, jagged ice, and chunks of cement left in the ground from a sewer project. In the darkness of the Bulgarian wilderness, the two brothers lay some sixty yards apart, with Bobo at the bottom of a deep ravine, torn up, bleeding badly, unable to move.

"My back was broken," said Bobo, from the table in the non-smoking section the day he told me the story. Our waitress, a woman of around fifty, with rugged facial skin like the underbelly of a rhino, refilled our water glasses.

"My brodder Jordan carry me on his back—hour at a time," Bobo looked at me while he spun his fork among his pasta primavera.

It was difficult for me to comprehend what this must have been like for the brothers. "Did they stop the train? Did they ever come after the two of you?"

"No. They figure we would die anyway. No one crosses Pirrin Mountains at that time of year. We were lucky; we made it through the mountains to Macedonia in five months."

"Did your back heal?"

"Once we get to Macedonia, we go to American embassy. From there, they fly Jordan and me to New York where I had to have surgery. The American coach prayed I would recover." Bobo put his fork down and dropped his head. I knew he was weeping. "Jordan try to save me. He lost three toes on his right foot from frost bite. His soccer career was over too."

I waited for a second. I didn't know what to say. We both sat silent, each with our own thoughts. The restaurant became so quiet; that I could hear forks and knives clinking against plate's ten tables away. The waitress started walking toward us with a coffee pot but I stopped her by putting my hand up and shaking my head no.

"Now's not a good time," I mouthed to her. She appeared to understand.

"I'm sorry Bobo," I said to him.

"Mario," Bobo choked out to me. "My brodder try to save me. All I hope for is I get big contract so I could pay him back. That was my dream. That was all I kept praying for while we were in the mountains."

That was 1977, the Americans just began to compete on the world level in soccer and they had desperately wanted Bobo to be their featured midfielder. The New York Nova, part of the now defunct American Soccer League, an upstart league who had signed a number of European and South American super-stars, wanted Bobo as well. Bobo was only thirty two and in his prime as a soccer player. The Nova club had made him an offer of over one-and-a-half million dollars per year.

It didn't end up that way. After the surgery, Bobo's playing days were over. Bobo told me that while he recuperated he felt he had aged by thirty years. Though Bobo and Jordan were successful in defecting from communist Bulgaria, Bobo's dream of playing in another World Cup as an American had ended with his fateful jump.

CHAPTER 2

I'M SECOND GENERATION Sicilian and Polish. My father had a short-lived professional boxing career in the early 1950's, and he made a name in the city circuits as a middleweight with a thunderous hand. His name was Frankie, but his nickname, "the Hitman,"—with less than subtle connotations, brought fear to every opponent. My father's hero was Rocky Marciano, the undefeated heavyweight champion of the world in the fifties. My father taught me Marciano's style of boxing from the time I could put gloves on. In our house, we lived for boxing. My father had no interest in any other sports.

I met Bobo Stoikov by chance eighteen years after he had settled in Michigan. Fred Castil, one of the fathers from the Rochester travel soccer team saw Luca play in a recreation game in the fall. On a Friday evening, sometime during the winter, Castil called asking if Luca could try out on Saturday at a Rochester gym for an open spot on the team. .

At the gym, Fred introduced me to Bobo, the team's trainer. Bobo put his hand out with his thumb up, making me clench his hand rather than the traditional handshake.

"How you do?" he said to me.

"Good. This is Luca."

I pointed to my son. Bobo touched Luca's face gently with his right hand. (At ten, Luca was almost as tall as Bobo.)

"I am Bobo. How you do?"

Luca smiled.

"Are you ready to play some soccer?" Bobo asked.

Luca nodded. Bobo grabbed his hand and pointed toward the other boys at the other side of the gym.

"Let's go over there," he told Luca.

I watched the two of them walk away. Bobo's legs were bowed like a cowboy at the rodeo.

The suburban gym was huge. I believe my entire high school could have fit inside it. There were four scoreboards high on the walls, above the school flags that represented every team in the Great Lakes Area conference. Off to the side and across the bleachers on the west side of the room was a small side gym, with two basketball nets, wrestling mats, and a gym rope.

Most gyms are loud, with sounds bouncing off the walls. With a rubber floor and blue mats covering all the walls, the sounds were muted inside the Hubbard Middle School gym. The player's parents stood beneath one of the baskets and casually spoke to each other. I noticed one skinny mother with shoulder length reddish hair and small breasts, tipping her sunglasses to look at me in an almost agitated way.

While Fred Castil and Mrs. Jansen, a team mother with an obscene amount of perfume on, talked about how excited they were to have Bobo as a trainer, I casually drifted away to watch Bobo's training session to see how his training session compared to those Luca had participated in with his recreation team. The drills seemed a lot different. I didn't see lines. I didn't see boys messing around. I didn't see boys wandering away from the session. All I could see was Bobo shuffling from side to side on the gym floor, playing perfect balls, from soft chip passes to through—balls with pace.

I heard Bobo constantly yelling, "Puurrrfect, puurrfect," or "Queeeck, queeeck," if he wanted the ball to move faster.

Luca fit in well. He made a couple of passes that led to easy goals. By the end of practice, Billy Castil had his arm around Luca's shoulder while another boy, Aaron Michaels, gave him a high-five.

After the other boys and their parents left, Bobo approached both Luca and me. "He's a midfielder. If he play in Europe, they pay him 50 million."

I had no idea what he was talking about. Bobo pointed with his right finger while cupping his left hand around Luca's head.

"To play the midfield, you must be a good person." He bent a little to look directly into Luca's eyes. "Midfielders don't ask for glory. They always sacrifice for sake of team. They give ball to all their teammates to score the goals." Bobo tilted his head. "Luca, you know the Bible?" he asked.

Luca nodded. "I go to catechism. We read the Bible there."

"Who then, the favorite apostle?"

I had no idea where Bobo was going with his story. Luca was confused as well.

"Who the favorite apostle?" Bobo asked again.

"Peter," Luca stated inquisitively.

"No! No!" Bobo said, raising his voice slightly, pushing his hands out in a bewildered manner. He looked up at me to make sure our eyes met. "It's OK," he said to Luca, touching his face again with his hand. "Peter is a defender—tough and strong. Judas is a striker. He play for himself." Bobo bent down to one knee. "Who was at the cross with Jesus?"

Luca looked at me, and then turned back at Bobo. He lifted his shoulders and raised his hands in gesture that showed he was just guessing. "Was it St. Michael?"

"Michael is an archangel. He not a man. Listen to me. I'll give you a hint."

Bobo put out his hand and showed four fingers to Luca.

"The Saint I'm speaking of wrote one of the Gospels."

Bobo used his fingers to count. "There was Luke, there was Mathew, there was…"

"St. John," Luca blurted out.

"Yes, yes, St. John was most like Jesus. When you out there today, you obey all the commandments of soccer. You never once steal ball from your teammate. You make all the right passes. Forward pass. Through pass. Back pass. Only a good person can make those passes."

The afternoon sunlight streamed into my eyes from small rectangular windows above the bleachers. I glanced at my watch. Bobo wasn't finished.

"If you are good person and you want to be the greatest of midfielders, then you must work hard to become St. John… St. John of the midfield."

The only way I could break up the intensity of that moment was to laugh. Bobo got a chuckle out of it as well while Luca stood there looking mystified. We were the only people left in the gym. I offered to take Bobo to lunch but he declined.

"I must get home to see my brodder," he told me.

CHAPTER 3

THE FOLLOWING DAY, which was Sunday, my wife Jenny, Luca, and I joined my parents, my uncles Angelo and Tony and their wives for Mass at St. John Vianney to commemorate the twentieth anniversary of my sister's death.

My sister Sofie had drowned at seventeen when the car she was a passenger in crashed through a guard rail on West River Road. Her boyfriend Jimmy Piccolo, the driver, had chugged a six pack of beer prior to the accident. He survived and lived a pretty good life for another five years or so. When he turned twenty four, when there would be little suspicion of retribution from my father, everyone in the neighborhood except me was stunned when Jimmy Piccolo took his own life with a drug overdose.

My name is Mario Santini. My father Frankie didn't have much choice about the destiny in he was given. His sacramental godfather was "Black Joe" Lotorri, the most infamous Detroit mafia don the State has ever known. I have a picture of my father, a black and white photo taken when he was about six, sitting on the knee of Black Joe, with his cousin Alphonso and his best friend Mazzie behind him in their dark wool suits.

Being my father's son, I didn't have much of a choice in what I wanted to do. After Chippewa Valley High School, he allowed me to go to college, but it had to be nearby. Knowing my career would be working for my father and uncles in their trucking business, I studied logistics and journalism for a couple of years at the local community college before earning my degree at Wayne State University in Transportation Management.

As the young CEO of Acer Packaging and Transportation company, my job was to coordinate the legitimate side of the family business. Stuck in a world where the only way out leads to being hunted down the rest of your life, for the sake of my family, and my father, I had no choice but to become the front for the organization. As a good son I handled our corporate accounts, moving freight back and forth on 53-foot dry box trailers between Laredo, Texas, and the Michigan automotive plants. I had a staff of thirty-five people, from operations personnel, to dock workers, craters, administrators, you name it—all housed inside our newly built terminal in New Boston, Michigan, a five-mile drive from the Romulus airport.

My father and uncles took care of the illegitimate side

of our business. Their job was to hide the marijuana, cocaine, and any other street drugs on our rigs, moving the product up from Mexico free of any transportation costs. They had their own men set up inside the mechanic's garage, a purposely dank and dirtied repair facility, set back two acres from our terminal. No one from my staff in the main office ever wanted to go to the repair facility. We used to say that dead people worked back there. Soon, the garage was known as the house of the living dead.

Of course I knew they were running an elaborate dope smuggling business, one which cartels around the world would be envious of. I told my father from the beginning I would have no involvement in that side of the business. Being half Polish disallowed me from being a "made man" in the family anyway. Deep down, without a doubt, I believe my father Frankie preferred it that way.

My father had married a Polish woman instead of a Sicilian woman so he could keep the nature of his business away from his wife. My mother had no idea what my father and his brothers were in to. She thought they were living in "Bridgewood,"—a small tranquil suburb in Clinton Township due to my father's modest salary he made running his modest trucking company. They would never have lived there if my father had a choice. He hated Bridgewood—where neighbors sprinkler systems seemed to be synchronized—where husbands and wives, stale from their cushy suburban lives, waved to be seen from other neighbors at the curbside, after lazily strolling in their robes to pick up the morning Free Press. As my fat Uncle Angelo told us a million times, "Bridgewood is the kind of place guys like us get sent to once we're in the Witness Protection Program."

If my mother had the money Frankie and his brothers counted in the basement after selling their dope, she could have lived in a palace.

After mass, my two uncles and aunts joined us at my parent's house for brunch. As soon as I arrived, my father took me in the kitchen to ask if a certain truck came in.

"Yes, yes," I told him. "How many times you gotta ask me?"

My father smiled, and then nodded to my two uncles, who immediately all put up their fists. As if on cue, the three of them dove into a shadow boxing routine, flinging haymakers all over the room until my mother started shaking a rolled up newspaper at them.

"Show some respect on such a solemn day," she told them. The three men snapped to attention like school boys, realizing the mistake they had made. Uncle Angelo made the sign of the cross. My father and my Uncle Tony followed his lead. They looked like altar boys praying in silence, heads tipped beneath a crucifix hanging above the table.

After my mother put the marinara sauce on the stove, the women went into the front room to talk and eat the pastries my mother had made. How I loved the smell of tomato sauce, slowly simmering in a pot, filling the entire kitchen with the aroma of oregano, onions, pepper, and other spices. Even though I was only half Sicilian, the smell was intoxicating to me.

Luca peeked into the kitchen with a "save me" look on his face.

"Go outside and kick the ball around," I told him.

My father overheard. "Get over here kid; come over here to your favorite grandpa." Luca walked to grandpa and leaned against him.

My dad put his hand out. "Look at that hand kid."

"Oh, no. Here we go," said Uncle Tony.

I too knew what was going on. My father loved to show off the size of his hands. They were twice the size of any of ours. It was like he was a freak of nature.

"How would you like to get hit with one of these, kid?"

"Leave him alone," said Tony.

"You want to get hit with one of them?" said my father to Tony.

Uncle Angelo was at the sink cutting up pepperoni and fontinella cheese. He was the oldest.

"Shuddupa the two of you, before I break all—a-your bones," he said in a fake Sicilian accent, actually mimicking the voice of their father, who made them laugh simultaneously. Uncle Angelo was the comedian of the family.

"You my flesh-n my blood. I'm a gonna have to do a number on you two guinea wops."

Frankie and Tony were revved up. They started speaking in the same accent to each other. Luca snuggled on to my father's lap. Angelo pushed all the pepperoni and cheese on to a wooden cutting board and placed it on the table.

"Mangia, mangia," he said. Luca quickly snatched a piece of cheese and put it in his mouth.

"Frankie, you see how quick that kid's hands are?" Tony said to my dad. My dad's eyes got real big.

"Oh no," I said to the two of them. "Don't even start. Luca's going to be a soccer player. Don't start him on the fighting stuff."

"Soccer? That's a sissy sport," my father replied." He stood up from the chair with Luca in his arms and placed him in the middle of the kitchen floor.

"Luca," he said. "Don't let your sissy dad start you on the wrong foot. What do you want to be, kid?"

Luca looked up at the ceiling and smiled. "Papa, I'm going to be a soccer player."

My father playfully pulled him close to him. My father was on his knees, with his arm around Luca and his forehead pushing on Lucas. "Maybe you didn't hear me buddy boy." Luca played along. My father circled his right arm behind him, ready to throw what he called a cartoon punch.

"Here comes the super-duper punch kiddo. I'll give you one more chance. Now what sport is it that you're gonna play?"

Luca pushed closer. Now both he and grandpa looked like two guys that were ready to go.

"I told you Papa, I'm gonna play soccer. My new coach Bobo says I'm gonna make 50 million."

My dad stopped his punch in mid circle. "50 million? Why didn't you tell me that kid? You make 50 million and you can do anything you want." My dad kissed Luca on the cheek. Then he lifted him up and put him on the counter. "Watch your daddy kid, watch what I taught him. You may be a soccer player, but to be a man, you must learn the greatest of sports."

It was show time. As a boy, I had performed the routine a thousand times for my uncles. I took off my shirt. My dad brought the gloves in from the laundry room, where several pairs always hung from hooks above the washer.

As he tightened them on my hands, he said to Luca, "Here we go Luca, if you want to be a great fighter; you have to know your history."

I got into my stance. My father began by calling out George Foreman's name. From there, I became the scowling George Foreman; I moved around the kitchen, shadow boxing with my hands high and open, like a girl playing patty-cake, pushing my opponent back, pushing him back, and hammering left and right hooks to his body. My father then called out "Smokin Joe Frazier" so I got on my toes, began bobbing my head up and down, started ducking, moving to my right to protect my bad eye, started throwing a round house left hook that could lift my opponent right off his feet.

Luca followed the action. Just like my uncles, his head and shoulders moved to the right and left as I postured around the kitchen in between the sink, the stove, and the table. When my father shouted Marciano, I crouched down like a man passing a kidney stone, reached my left arm out to measure where my opponent was, and then when close enough, I started wailing right and left upper cuts to my imaginary foe's body, punches which would suck the breath right out of a man and then my father shouted Joe Louis, so I was back up in a classical stance, head high like a regal king, slowly inching forward, zinging my opponent with quick left jabs until I could clock him with my powerful right.

"Give me Tommy Hearns," shouted my father.

I let my legs wobble like the scarecrows in the Wizard of Oz. Luca laughed. With my right hand close to my chin, just waiting to pounce, I started firing left jabs with the speed and precision of a lizard's tongue.

I had a good sweat going. It was time for a little more comedy so my father, always the showman, called out Mike Tyson's name. My uncles, who of course were part of the act, immediately put their hands over their ears. I snarled, went over to Luca sitting on the kitchen counter, and faked like I was a cannibal trying to chomp off the top of his ears.

Luca knew who Mike Tyson was so he too covered up, crying out, "No daddy, don't bite me, don't bite me."

"Now show Tyson some respect," my father stated on cue. Immediately, I brought my gloves in over my face, twisted my hands inward, and took my imagined opponent to the corner where the sink and the counters came together and started hitting him with right and left combinations, swinging my hands with equal power.

"Now give him the double," ordered my father. I sent my right into the midsection of my opponent, and then pushed my right up in one sweeping upper cut motion to the chin.

"He's the only one I ever saw do that, "said my father in awe. I winked at my dad, letting him know I was getting winded, letting him know it was time for the show's finale.

"Muhammad Ali," my father cried, like a ring master at the circus.

I started dancing, hopping around the kitchen as light on my feet as Fred Astaire, beating my chest with my right glove, "I'm the greatest of all time," I shouted. "I'm pretty, I've never been hit."

With my feet, I dazzled the crowd of three by doing the "Ali shuffle." I could see that Luca was impressed.

"I shook up the world, I shook up the world," I repeated a couple of times. I started head hunting, flicking quick jab after jab to my opponent's face, dancing to my left, side-stepping punches, launching three or four combinations in quick successive attacks.

Finally I stopped. "I need water", I cried. I turned on the cold water and drank directly from the faucet to the sound of my uncles and Luca clapping their hands.

My wife Jenny came into the kitchen.

"We need help. Mom is crying again," she said.

"Oh no," said my father, sarcastically. "I hope she's not seeing dead Polish people again."

CHAPTER 4

I SENT EVERYONE HOME, including Jenny and Luca so I could spend some time alone with my mother. My track record was pretty good for being able to calm her down.

With my father snoring from the couch in the family room, I sat with my mother Marzena in her "blue" room, which was the converted bedroom of my sister Sofie. After Sofie's death, it was particularly difficult for my mother to be in this room, but over time, it became my mother's sanctuary. It was where she went to think, rest, and pray. The room was painted light sky blue, with thick white crown molding around the top which blended into the white ceiling.

Water color portraits of my sister hung on the wall. A well known local artist, Al Ochsner, painted the pictures from photographs my mother had given him. In a darker blue hue, thin French moldings framed the four paintings.

In the corner, a simple book shelf became a shrine. The top shelf held four candles, a wooden sculpture of baby Jesus, Joseph, and Mary on a donkey, an icon of St. Joseph holding Jesus, and a photo of John Paul II holding his hand across his forehead in a contemplative pose.

Above the shrine, were copies of artwork depicting the passion of Jesus, Mary's assumption, and a portrait of Mother Teresa.

"This is how I want my room in heaven to look," my mother told me. When she uttered that sentence, I knew it wouldn't be long before she asked me how I wanted my room to look. I was prepared.

"Mr. Mario," she said as she grabbed my hand. "Tell me how you want your room to look again."

"My dear mother," I said solicitously. "My room is spacious, and airy, with the walls made up of pure white marble. A gentle breeze tickles white sheers from an open balcony, pushing them across the floors like foamy waves at a beach. A small fire crackles in my fireplace. Through a crystal clear window in front of me, I can see the Mediterranean Sea, its coastline, and its horizon, where the light blue of the sky greets the dark blue green of the sea."

"That's so poetic."

It better be I thought to myself. I had been saying it to her for over ten years.

My mother suffered from depression, heart

palpitations, anxiety attacks and other psychological disorders. Her problems began right after I was born, when her post partum blues had been so extreme she was put on suicide watch. She recovered for awhile, enough time to take care of me as a toddler. When I was four years old, she made her first visit to Glen Eden, an asylum for the mentally ill.

"You got your passion from your father," my mother said to me. "Thank God you got your compassion from me, the Polish side."

"It balances me out mother."

"If you were a full-blooded Sicilian you'd be an animal."

"You've told me that a million times."

"But it's true."

My parents were an odd couple. Pa was dark with his olive colored skin, his hair still thick and dark like Dean Martin's, and though he gained weight from his fighting days, he still maintained a good shape for a man in his late fifties.

My mother's skin was paler than some of the ghosts she swore she saw. She was a smaller woman, just a nip over five feet and had a pear shape, where most of the weight she gained fell to her rear-end.

She was the brains of the family. As a young student, she had been promoted twice through high school, graduating at the age of sixteen. Back then, even for a woman with such a high intellect, opportunities were slim for women. My mother ended up being a waitress and a secretary until she became pregnant with Sofie. In the back of my mind, I always felt it was my mother's unfulfilled potential that set her back.

Frankie was definitely no intellectual. Just trying to complete the simplest of crossword puzzles, he'd continuously call out the clue to mother so she could supply him with the appropriate word. Even though my mother answered half the questions, pa always put the puzzle down after finishing it like he conquered the intellectual world. I recall as a kid, pa flopping the paper down. "Those damn bastards," he said. "Did they think they could fool a Santini?"

When I was fourteen, my mother returned from her latest visit to Glen Eden. She was resting while my father was in the basement with his brothers counting money and cleaning their guns. I recalled hearing my father complain, "Why I married her I'll never know. If she was Sicilian, Mario would have been the greatest middle weight of all time."

Uncle Angelo responded, "Frankie, science has proven there is no intellect housed in the head of a penis."

Uncle Tony snickered. "Yeah, Yeah, you got spell bound with Marzena's large Polish tits."

The three of them started laughing.

"It gave Frankie one stiff kielbasa," said Angelo.

Now they were roaring.

"Never under estimate what a big pair of jugs will do to a man," said Uncle Angelo, laughing so hard he sounded like he was crying, spitting out the words.

Even though my father's secret life was hidden from my mother, he was still a difficult man to live with. He was violent, so quick to fight. Though he did everything he could to fit into the peaceful neighborhood, sometimes, his temper got the better of him.

Once, when Sofie and I were little kids, my father was outside talking to a television repairman named Saputo. A small man, Saputo always wore a baseball cap and thick black glasses that made him look like a mad scientist. Sofie and I were kneeling on the couch, looking outside through the living room picture window.

In those days, a TV repairman would drive up and down the streets of the suburb, pulling his trailer with his truck, picking up sets that needed work and delivering the TV's that were repaired.

Saputo had already been to our house twice without fixing the TV to my father's satisfaction. From the window, Sofie and I could see Saputo and my father speaking with their hands. When my father pulled his hands close to him with his thumbs and index fingers stuck together, I sensed something was coming. Sure enough, my father flung an overhand right that Saputo couldn't avoid. It broke Saputo's nose while opening a gash between his eye and the bridge of his nose.

"Mommy, mommy," Sofie shouted, "Daddy's fighting again, Daddy's fighting again."

My mother ran out the front door with a dish rag to help Saputo clean up his face. Saputo held himself up by bracing his hand against the tree on our boulevard, his glasses cockeyed on his face.

My father was known to dole out his own brand of justice. Another time, we stopped to watch my Uncle Tony play in a softball game at Fraser Park. Uncle Tony was at second base trying to complete a double play throw back to first. My father thought one of the players from Continental Plastics slid too roughly into Tony and he started to razz the other team's players, making fun of their neon green shirts.

"You look like a bunch of sissies," he shouted from the top of the softball bleachers.

The ump tossed us out. Uncle Tony came out of the dugout and gave my father a look that suggested you would have to be an idiot to start a fight over something so stupid.

We stopped at old man Miceli's bowling alley at the corner of Garfield and 14 Mile Road and waited for Tony to show after the game. My father finished a pitcher of beer and I downed two sugary colas as we sat in the lounge watching the Tiger baseball game on a small TV over the bar.

Pretty soon, nature called. The men's room at

Miceli's was tight for space. Even as a small boy I had to squeeze in between the two urinals, toilets, and the sink. As my father was relieving himself at the first urinal, the door opened, and from the corner of my eye I saw a wall of neon green enter. My father saw it as well. The poor guy unfortunately brushed against my father who figured the guy was there to start some trouble. Before the player could unzip himself, my father's fists came out in full force, hitting him with more combinations than were thrown in the Hearns-Hagler fight. The ball player, who was a moose of a man, couldn't fight back. He ended up against the sink, with his hands protecting his face while Frankie leveled body shots to his sides.

When the guy fell to the floor, his head hit the back of the sink and it knocked him out. Frankie grabbed my hand.

"Let's get the hell out of here," he shouted.

Nothing compared with my favorite Frankie moment. A young punk named Al Taylor moved back to live with his parents who owned the last house on our street. He immediately started giving my buddies and me a hard time when we passed his house on the way to school.

Over six feet tall and easily three hundred pounds, Taylor dressed like a beatnik. His hair was long and oily and he had a peach fuzz beard—probably to hide his acne. Taylor drove a souped up light blue LeSabre and liked to race the engine when he came down South Wind Drive. The bully especially enjoyed scaring and scattering the kids who were playing in the street.

During a time when my mother was at Glen Eden, my father and I were working on the lawn on a hot Saturday afternoon. Sofie was on the porch with a glass of lemonade. It seemed as though the entire neighborhood was out working—transistor radios were on the porch steps of every house, the legendary play-by-play man Ernie Harwell fired off his signature line, "it's loong goone!" as soon as the ball cracked off of Sweet Lou Whitaker's bat. The three-run Tiger homer brought a roar of applause to the street.

My father was raking grass clippings in the street at the curb of the boulevard when I heard an engine roar from a car still out of my view. I figured it had to be Taylor since he was the only jerk who would try to pick up speed while going down a residential street.

Sure enough it was him. The noise of the engine was so cranked up it sounded like a low-flying jet. He must have been going 45 miles per hour as he headed toward our straight away.

The other fathers stopped what they were doing to watch and to make sure their kids were safe. Not my father. He didn't look up; he just kept on raking apparently oblivious to Taylor's grandstanding.

As soon as Taylor passed our mailbox, my father let go of his rake similar to a farmer tossing his pitchfork.

The rake handle jetted through the air entering the open window of Taylor's LeSabre and struck him in the face.

Taylor squeezed down on the brakes. The car skidded and swerved. In a frantic second or two, Taylor furiously spun his steering wheel from side to side to straighten the car out. He ended up on old man Drennan's lawn, clipping the mailbox with the back end of his car.

Taylor flung his car door open and sprung from his seat like a WWF wrestler ready to inflict some serious pain to Frankie. "Prepare to die old man," were his words as he swaggered toward my father in his tight blue jeans and black pointed boots.

Frankie stood his ground. When Taylor stood about ten feet from Frankie, he started a typical freak punch routine, where, for some reason, the inexperienced street fighter gets on one foot and starts skipping toward his opponent, picking up speed, holding his right hand at the side of his chest, ready to unload it into the face of his unsuspecting target.

But my father was a former professional fighter. He warned me a million times never to telegraph my punches, never to be predictable when throwing an over-hand right. When Taylor threw the most obvious punch in the history of boxing, my father simply ducked, let Taylor's momentum take him by, and pivoted his feet quickly so he could uncork a left hand upper cut into Taylor's midsection. I was surprised Frankie's hand didn't come out grasping Taylor's liver.

Taylor lurched forward, exposing his face. A quick and tight right hand to the chin was all that was needed to knock him out. He dropped to his knees and tumbled backwards until he settled in the middle of the South Wind Drive.

Standing over Taylor's massive body for over a minute, Frankie became aware of all the neighborhood spectators. In a spontaneous celebration, the crowd clapped in approval, hailing Frankie as the savior of the neighborhood. Six packs of beer started making their way over to our house from the men on the street. I've never seen Frankie drink that much in my entire life.

* * *

As shadows cast themselves across the room, my mother grabbed my right hand and clutched it between her two tiny sweaty palms.

"Will you and Jenny try to have another baby?" she asked.

"We're trying mother."

"I hope so. I hope you have a girl."

"If we do, we're going to name her Sofie."

"That's so exciting! That would be such an honor! Make sure you spell it the Polish way."

"Yes, it will be Sofie with an F, not Sophie, or Sophia with the PH."

"You're a good son."

"I'm your only son."

She smacked my hand and smiled. Then she looked away.

"What if the ghost comes to see me tonight?" she asked.

"Tell him Mario says hello."

"Seriously," she protested, with a frightened look on her face.

"Stay close to Pops. No ghost is going to want to mess with him—especially when he's snoring."

"You sound like Uncle Angelo with all these foolish jokes."

"I'm tired Mama. I've got to get home to Jenny and Luca."

CHAPTER 5

AT THE TEAM barbeque in late May, I was asked to be the assistant coach for Bobo and the Rochester Crusaders for their upcoming season. I was stunned to say the least, since I didn't know much about the game. The previous assistant coach, Paul Hermodi, announced he had been asked by his company to transfer to Florida. Fred Castil told me I was Bobo's choice. Jenny laughed hysterically, knowing I was petrified about trying to teach something I knew nothing about. She kept teasing me, referring to me as "Coach" the entire afternoon.

We started in July. Bobo set the practices up at Delia Park, a municipal facility in Sterling Heights that had four fields. Bobo told the parents the first two weeks would be optional practices, as he understood many of the families took vacations at that time of the year.

Every day, ten to twelve players showed up. I was glad Jenny didn't see me in my coaching position or

I would never have heard the end of it. At first, I was merely the ball fetcher, the guy who sits behind the net, chasing balls from errant shots before they are lost in the woods or stuck under a car in the parking lot. I excelled at dropping orange cones wherever Bobo pointed to, and separating from Bobo's bag, the multi colored practice bibs from Bobo's bag for scrimmages. At the end of practice, I was the guy who cleaned up all the Gatorade and half-filled water bottles scattered on the sidelines.

Little by little, from just being around Bobo and the boys, I started to learn the game. Soon, I could see the ball needed to be played from side to side on the field, not just forward.

Bobo constantly shouted during the scrimmages, "Sweeeetch, sweeetch the field," letting the boys know he wanted the ball to shift to the other side in order to catch the opposing team with a shortage of defenders.

I also learned the importance of dribbling skills. Bobo told us at the beginning of the mini-camp that each player had to become a polished jewel, that each player had to be able to possess the ball well, create space on his own, had to have the ability to beat a defender under difficult circumstances to score a goal.

That's why during the first forty-five minutes of every practice Bobo concentrated his training on the development of foot skills. He showed the boy's one move after another—from step-over's to scissor moves, telling the boys to choose freely amongst the moves that they as individuals, felt most comfortable with.

"Cannot play like robot. Must have individual cree-a-tivity," he stated at every practice.

More than anything, I learned it was a good thing to possess the ball for long periods of time. As a spectator, it frustrated me to see the players passing the ball around the back half of the field instead of kicking it down field toward the other team's goal. Bobo explained to all of us the importance of possession during a water break.

"Boys listen. Game is like a chess match. Professional teams knock the ball around, move it to all sides of the field. Why they do that?"

Luca put his hand up. Bobo nodded at him.

"To tire the other team out?"

"Not bad," Bobo said and continued. "Professional teams are looking for the other team's weakness. They must find the weak link of the other team and expose it."

As the boys and I lifted our hands to our eyes to shield the sun, Bobo lifted a ball.

"Let me introduce you to the game. It is the ball. It never gets tired. Loook, loook, at all of you, sweating, faces so red you look like you gonna explode. When you become a team, the ball does all the work. Someday, you will become so good; you can order pizza on field while the other team chases the ball."

We all laughed. So did Bobo, whose head jiggled when he laughed.

There was no doubt the team was getting better with Bobo's training. It was also obvious how much Luca loved playing soccer, how much he loved being taught by Bobo. Our house became Luca's secondary training facility. He practiced his soft passing against our couch; juggled his ball in the kitchen while watching TV, or boomed shot after shot against the kitchen's outside brick wall until Jenny went mad from the noise.

Luca insisted he be dropped off at practice at least a half hour ahead of the other boys. He knew Bobo was always there early, setting up the goals and corner flags. Once the training field was set, Bobo and Luca practiced together until the other boys straggled in, working on difficult feint moves, learning how to pass a ball with the side of his foot, trying to master the technique to hit a soft chip pass with back spin.

And before every practice, I watched what I told Jenny was the "Bobo and Luca show," two crazed soccer fanatics who lived for the game and fed off each other. Luca loved to hear Bobo say, "puuurrfect, puuurfect", after he did something Bobo felt was at a high level, or best of all, was when Bobo would walk toward me, his head rocking, Slavic eyes squinting, his smile exposing some missing teeth, just to tell me loud enough for Luca to hear, "Mario. Someday Luca gonna play for 50 million."

Jenny called Bobo's expressions "Bobo'isms." For instance, if he saw a player who he felt was big and stiff he would say, "He moves like a refrigerator being pushed across the kitchen floor."

If he was trying to express the importance for a player to have field vision he would say, "Architect look at an empty field and already see what he is going to build." My particular favorite saying was when Bobo would assess someone who had no chance of making the team. "Mario," he would say discreetly, "I cannot make chicken soup out of chicken shit."

His stories were even better. I learned that one of the common mistakes young players make is to take the ball back into pressure, the place from which they had just freed the ball from. Rather than yell at our players, Bobo took them aside to tell them a story he hoped would open their minds to the danger of bringing the ball back to the defender.

"If a house is on fire and you are walking down the street and you hear mother cry, help, save my baby, what you do?"

All the boys agreed they would run in the house to save the baby.

"OK," said Bobo. "Now you have the baby in your arms. You take it outside away from the burning house to the street. Under any condition, would you take the baby back into the burning house?"

The boys shook their head. "Of course not," said

Pepe, a Mexican boy who had just moved up from the second team.

"Then why you do it with the ball?" The boys looked dumbfounded. Bobo pointed to them, "Keep the baby safe from the burning house."

In our first tournament game, after taking a commanding 6-0 lead, Luca mentioned to his fellow midfielder to remind those behind him to keep the baby out of the burning house. It didn't take long for the entire team to repeat the order. Within minutes every player was telling his nearest teammate to keep the baby out of the burning house. It got to the point they were literally screaming. The other team was confused. The referee was confused. More than anyone, our parents were confused.

"What the fuck is going on out there," Fred whispered in my ear.

"I can't explain it, just another Boboism," I told him.

Michigan winters inevitably come early. On postcards, or on marketing brochures issued by the State, winter is always displayed as a happy time, where children frolic in powdery snow, and lovers skate on ice-ponds with a glass like sheen, families sleigh or ski in the rugged snow filled terrain of the great white north.

Instead, the winters I had known were filled with slush and wet snow caked around tractor tires, drenched in mud and motor oil, freezing rain that veered my tractor trailers right off the slicked down freeways into ditches, and every February, an arctic blast of air so cold it could freeze a truck's radiator and my mechanic's nose right off his face.

By late November, with winter casually introducing itself, soccer teams headed for indoor facilities to continue their playing or training. And, it was no different for us. Bobo's team played in a league at a facility in Fraser, playing on a boarded field with six players and a goalie.

Ahead by 6-2 at the half, Bobo wasn't happy with the way the team was playing. When the boys came off the field, they squirted their mouths with water or Gatorade and sat down on the turf field with their backs against the wall. Bobo waited for all of them to quiet down.

"You are losing 2-0," he told them. Pepe and Alex pointed to the scoreboard.

"No Bobo, look at the scoreboard," Pepe said to him. Bobo raised his right hand, put it up to his mouth and gave them the universal sign of zipping their mouths closed.

"You are losing 2-0. They score two very nice goals. All you score are garbage goals... you steal ball and shoot off boards; somebody picks up rebound like garbage man in front of goal and kicks it in. I can get my grandmother to do that."

Bobo turned to me and winked. "I want the ball to move around the field—boom, boom, boom," Bobo said, lifting his knee like he was passing a ball.

"You can only score after making seeex passes. If I think the goal is a good one I will let you know. Now get out there and play like I have taught you."

The boys quickly found out Bobo meant what he said. After stealing the ball from the other team off a goal kick and whacking it in, Billy Castil glanced over at Bobo who was leaning over the boards. Bobo shook his head no.

"Not a goal. Need to have seeex passes."

I stood on the same side as the players near the mid field line. About ten minutes into the half, with the restrictions Bobo put on them, the team figured out to move the ball from side to side, then back, maybe forward, then across to an open teammate. Bobo even forced them to play the ball back to Aaron Michaels, the keeper, who Bobo claimed had the touch of a construction worker.

"Its like he's got dried cement all around his work boots," Bobo said, smiling, his head bopping up and down while he chuckled.

Soon, after every goal, the boys would look over at Bobo the way the Romans had looked at the emperor for his hand signal that would determine who would live or die. If Bobo liked the goal, he would simply nod. If the goal didn't live up to Bobo's expectations, he would look away from the boys and sip his coffee.

At the end of that game, Bobo took the boys into the

corner, under an electric heater that radiated so much warmth; I secretly wished Bobo's post game speech would be a short one.

"Boys. I don't care about the score. I care about how you play. Today, you play against cones. It's not their fault. Their coach does not work with them enough. Your mothers, playing in their high-heels could have won this game."

Some of the boys were wrestling their warm-up pants over their shoes. Others sat back against their bags that lined the outer walls of the field house. But they all listened attentively to what Bobo said. "What is important for you to understand, the game must be played the right way. We cannot afford to start bad habits. Just keeecking the ball down the field is not the answer. You must be composed. You must see your passing outlets two moves ahead. You must always be in a position to support your teammate. If you cannot do that, then… you must take up the tuba and play in the school band."

All the boys laughed. Luca mimicked like he was playing a tuba. He caught my eye and smiled.

Going into the winter season, the team was in the middle of the pack in league play. By spring, after the continued and comprehensive training program during the winter, the team had a great season winning the league easily and going undefeated in tournament play. At the club banquet, our team was announced as a "team to watch." In just a couple of years, the boy would become eligible to play in the State Cup Championships. The club president, Jeff Hopper, remarked that our team was the "team of the future." Bobo, the parents, and the boys were elated by the praise. After the speech, at the bar holding two glasses filled with beer, Fred Castil told me he felt so good he was going to start dancing in the aisles."

CHAPTER 6

WHEN THE ROCHESTER Crusaders were a middle-of-the-pack team, they were not considered a threat. Coaches from other teams would shake Bobo's and my hands prior to the game or chat about other teams in the league. They even made small talk about the wonderful things we were doing with the development of our players. It wasn't unusual for them to ask if we were interested in playing "friendly" scrimmages in upcoming tournaments at their fields.

As long as we were not a threat to knock a team from their perch, we were good guys. However, after the terrific season we ended up having, the warm amiable greeting was officially over. The change started at the league registration meeting.

Bobo pulled me aside. "Mario. Why everybody staring at us?"

"I don't know. It looks like a few of them are frothing

at the mouth."

"It feels like their eyes are right on me."

Fred Castil pulled us aside. "Fuck'-em all boys. Now that we're good, we're wearing a target on our backs."

Being a novice, I had no idea how competitive people were with youth soccer. That changed when I received a call from Andy Mayer, the coaching director of one of the top clubs in the state. He was a local coaching legend who had founded his youth club the Raiders twenty-five years earlier. He was also the head coach of the men's soccer team at my alma mater Wayne State University.

We met mid afternoon at Missouri Macs, a trendy suburban bar outside an indoor soccer facility in Troy. Andy finished up a meeting with his coaching staff, then grabbed a half-filled pitcher of beer from the table and joined me at one of the high stool counters in the corner of the room near the pool tables.

"You need to join us," he said to me right out of the box.

"Join your club?" I asked.

"I've watched your son. He's a great player. He needs to play with boys of his own ability."

Every dad likes hearing a compliment about his kid. I admit I felt a little pride glowing inside of me. Then I came to my senses.

"What is it you want from me?"

"I want you to bring your son and four of your best players, Pazquez, Morrison, Liddle, and Castil's kid to the Raiders. We'll have a team that's a sure bet to win the state cup next year."

Mayer was heavy-set guy, with a silver-spiked crew cut and a face rounder than a pumpkin. In the brief time that I met him, he seemed like a guy who could talk about himself all day. What annoyed me was that he constantly kept peeking at himself in a mirror over my shoulder, the way a weightlifter does who romances himself after every repetition.

"Face it," he told me. "The Raiders are the best club in the State—one of the best Clubs in America. We were just ranked number four by Soccer America magazine."

I had no reason to doubt him but I shook my head, "Castil would never come to you. He's on the board of the Rochester club. He's not going anywhere. The rest of the team Bobo and I control."

Mayer filled our glasses and then inched closer by pushing his head across the table. "I'll even let Bobo coach the team for another year." Mayer pulled back in his seat and glared at me. He took his left hand and knocked it casually against the table. "What do you think about those apples?"

"All I can do is to talk to Bobo and the group you want. It will be their decision."

"Remember, the kids who play for the Raiders make the Olympic development teams, they play in the national finals, and when they get to about sixteen or seventeen, they're the ones who get the free rides to the major universities. The Rochester Crusaders is a rinky-dink club. Outside of your team, name me one team that they have that's good?"

"I'm new to all of this," I told him. "I have no clue as to who is good and who isn't. I'm just trying to help my kid play the sport he loves."

Andy Mayer held out his hand. "Give me a call when you have an answer. Remember, I have a pretty good track record."

* * *

That evening, after telling Jenny about my meeting with Mayer, she told me to contact Bobo right away and meet with him. She didn't like the idea of us leaving the club; she was against us changing in any way.

"We have friends on the team now, we just can't walk away from them," she told me before I called Bobo.

Bobo's mini-van was in the shop, so I picked him up at his apartment across town, almost thirty miles away. He lived in Plymouth, on the west side, in a small one bedroom apartment in an apartment village called "Bournemouth."

Bobo's living room was a shrine to soccer. On the walls were photos of teams he had played with in Bulgaria and teams he trained once he came to America.

"I had lot more hair back then," said Bobo, pointing

to a picture of him squatting in the front row with the starting eleven of the Bulgarian national team.

"Yes, you did. You almost had an afro," I told him, thinking to myself, it was a bad afro. Bobo pointed to another player standing in the back row.

"That's my brodder Jordan. We play together for six years on national team."

"What position did he play?"

"He a defender. He play like a butcher. I tell him I'm the beauty, and he was the beast."

The only player I recognized as I glanced at over a hundred photos on the wall was Pele, the greatest player of all time, standing next to Bobo in a black and white photo with the year '66 written in the corner.

"Even I know who that guy is," I said to Bobo.

"I play against him in '66 in an international friendly. I score one, he score two. They win 2-1. He's a good guy."

The last photo on the wall before Bobo's bedroom caught my attention. Bobo was standing next to a young woman while holding a baby in his arms.

"Who is that?" I asked, pointing at the woman.

"That is my wife."

"Then that is your son."

"Yes. She left me a year after the picture was taken."

"Sorry Bobo. I'm sorry to hear that."

"It's OK."

"Do you mind me asking where they are now?"

"She moved somewhere to Cal–ee-fornia. I haven't seen them for over ten years."

Looking at Bobo, I could tell he was becoming uneasy, I knew I had to shift the conversation away from his family. I pointed to his large-screen television. "Is that thing big enough Bobo?"

Bobo immediately grinned.

"Mario. I get all the games from around the world. I have the Dish network here. I tape all the games and watch them over and over."

"And what's that in the corner?" I could see it was a massaging chair.

"That's my life-line. With my bad back, I need to seeet in the chair two to three times per day. It's got three speeds of vibration. Come, seeet in it, I'll show you."

"No, no," I told him. "If I sit in that, I'll never want to get up and we'll never get out in time to eat. I'll try it some other time."

Bobo wanted to go to the Amez Brothers family restaurant, which he told me was his favorite place to eat.

"They have a lot of soft food on the menu. It's hard for me to chew," he told me in the car, pointing to the three or four good teeth he had left on his bottom gums.

When I told him about the proposal on the table from the Raiders, Bobo immediately became upset.

"No.No. Never go to Raiders," he fumed, pounding his fist with his fork held upright on the table. "Mario, they play "smash mouth soccer" over at Raiders. They are nothing but keeeck and run teams, boot the ball down the field and run after it like a bunch of monkeys."

"I'm glad you think that way Bobo, because Jenny and I don't want to leave."

"Mario, we are building something special. We are teaching the game as it was intended to be played."

"I understand, I understand. I simply wanted to tell you what happened. It's my obligation to tell you what goes on."

"Andy Mayer is a thief in the night. He never develop any player. He steals players after somebody else does all the work!"

It took an hour to calm Bobo down. It was rare for him to show any kind of emotion. After spending two hours with him at the restaurant, I learned that he had coached for Andy Mayer twelve years earlier, putting together a national cup team for the Raiders. He told me Andy Mayer had taken the team away from him right before the season started so Andy could coach the team.

"He stole it away from me Mario, just so he can say he won national title."

"Were you his assistant then?"

"No, no. He sent me down to work with an eight-year old team, to develop them. At the end of the year, he sent me job hunting."

On the ride back to Bobo's tiny apartment, he thanked me for making soccer fun to coach again. He enjoyed the fact that Fred and I took care of all the off-the-field matters, allowing him to do what he loved the most—to train and to coach the boys.

"Mario. I'm no good with the parents. Can't deal with all their demands."

I pulled up in front of Bobo's place. After he fidgeted with the seatbelt, unsuccessfully unlocking it two or three times, a desperate yet sorrowful expression came across his face.

"Mario, all I have is soccer. It's what I live for. Please don't let them take it away from me again. I don't need trophies. All I care about is getting one player to the top... then I die in peace."

After watching Bobo sluggishly walk away, and recalling my conversation with Andy Mayer, I wondered, as I drove home, if the rest of my time spent in youth soccer was going to be complicated by off the field politics. With a sense of reservation, I continued home, funneling through the turns and overpasses of 696, wondering what exactly it was I got myself into.

When I returned home, all Jenny wanted to talk about was the picture I'd mentioned to her about Bobo's wife.

"I can't believe he was married," she said. "He's never mentioned it to any of us."

"Some people keep things private, to themselves."

"Did you ask him what her name was, what his son's name was?"

"No. Guys don't do that stuff. Women ask questions like that."

Jenny rolled her eyes.

"What? Am I wrong? Did you want me to ask him when he was having his periods, who he's sleeping with, and what cream works best on his yeast infections?"

"Oh God, you're sick," she replied back to me. "You guys are all afraid to ask questions. That's why you're always lost."

Jenny snuck into the bathroom while I took off my shirt in our walk-in closet. By the time I could get my shoes off, she was smiling in excitement at the open door.

"Hurry, hurry, you brute. I'm ovulating." She cried out to me. "Get your ass in here."

Just hearing the word, "ovulating" was a turn off for me when it came to making love. Men spend their entire lives prior to marriage, hoping a woman will beg you to make love to her. Then, when you're married and your naked wife is beckoning you to bed like a French whore, for some reason, when the word ovulating is mentioned, it's difficult for a man to get excited. I felt like I was in a clinic, performing a duty so some technician could run an experiment on me. Still, I did my duty that day. Shortly after we were finished, Luca knocked on the door.

"What's wrong?" Jenny asked while opening the door.

"I heard sounds. I'm scared."

Jenny turned around and gave me the "way-to-go" sign.

"You're an animal just like your father," she mumbled to me, as she walked by me on the way to the bathroom.

"I can't help I'm Sicilian below the waist—where it counts, "I quietly replied.

I looked at Luca. Before I could ask him a question he crawled in our bed. He'd spent the day with my mother and father and came home while I was meeting with Bobo at the restaurant.

"How was Grandpa Frankie today," I asked him, as I put my left arm around him and pulled him toward me. I puffed up a few pillows and then leaned back.

"He was funny. He showed me how to box."

"Really?"

"Yeah. I couldn't get to the refrigerator unless I boxed him to it."

"That's the oldest trick in his book. That's how he taught me."

I was glad Jenny was in the bathroom. She didn't need to hear Luca telling how grandpa was turning him into a monster.

"Did he throw any fake fruit at you?"

Luca gave me a baffled look.

"Fruit, He didn't throw any fruit."

"Never mind..."

My father used to throw an array of plastic fruit at me whenever he was mad. The fruit was on the kitchen table, in a wooden bowl that served as a table setting. If I didn't feel like boxing him or didn't put the energy into the match he thought I should, he would grab the artificial pieces and throw them as hard as he could at me while I covered up in the corner of the kitchen.

The apple was always the first to be hurled. It was the hardest and did the most damage. Next to slam against my back were the orange, then the pear, then the banana. All he had left in his arsenal after that were the grapes, which were spongy and soft.

Grandma and grandpa took me for ice cream."

"What did you have?"

"You know. What I always get, chocolate peanut-butter."

Jenny came out of the bathroom. She looked at me and smiled. Her fingers were crossed. She practically leaped into the bed, snuggling up to Luca who was in between the two of us.

"Luca, make sure you pray that Mommy can have another baby."

"I always do."

"What do you want us to pray for you to have Luca?," Jenny asked. I impersonated Bobo's voice, straining my vocal chords to get the right sound.

"He want to play for 50 million."

Jenny looked at me.

"Don't quit your day job," she said.

Luca put his head down on my stomach and yawned. Jenny tickled the back of his neck, lifting his blond hair away so her fingers had more room to stroke.

"What is it Luca you want us to pray for?" Jenny asked again.

"I want to become St. John... St. John of the midfield," he said, just loud enough for both of us to hear before he closed his eyes and drifted into sleep.

Jenny gazed at me with a worried look. I mouthed the words, "I'll tell you the story tomorrow." Jenny nodded like she understood, then put her head down on her pillow and fell asleep as well.

CHAPTER 7

WE HAD THE best tryout in the history of the Rochester Crusader club. In the first year, only fifteen players tried out. Going into our second year, sixty-three players tried to earn a spot on a sixteen player roster. Prospective players came from north of Saginaw, and as far west as Grand Rapids and Kalamazoo.

Somehow, Fred Castil found out about the Raiders making overtures about his son, mine, and a few others. He told me how worried he was about Luca possibly making a move to our arch rival. He was down right giddy about Bobo and me turning down Andy Mayer.

"This is just great," he kept repeating, while we stood by the cyclone fence separating the two fields. "Should I order the hardware now?"

"What hardware?"

"The trophies we're going to win next year for taking the state cup."

"We're a year away from that. A year is a long time."

"Are you kidding me? With the talent out there, winning the cup is a shoo-in."

The reality struck me. The soccer community included all types of individuals. Those who had to win at all costs, those who seemed to be there just so they could talk about their son, those who would watch every single practice, scrimmage or game as if the team was participating in the World Cup.

The more I got to know Fred Castil, the more I realized what an odd fellow he was. He was a short guy who carried his weight like Jell-O shaking outside the bowl. He had what I call a fluff fat, a heaviness starting right under his ears and draping down until it gathered in one rather wobbly shaped basketball beer gut, right above his belt buckle. As I talked, Fred often looked past me in an empty gaze. He would sneak a peak at me only from the corner of his eye that was nearest me, otherwise looking toward a horizon or event occurring in the distance. He always gave me the impression he wasn't interested in a word I was saying, until of course, I mentioned his son's name, and then he was all ears.

Mocking Fred, I once suggested he might consider having his own cable show on his son's soccer career. Standing among a few of the parents on the team, Fred didn't catch the verbal jab, even when the group of parents nearby laughed under their breath and nodded in agreement.

Every conversation with Fred led back to the topic of his son. If you discussed the weather, Fred would interject a story of his son Billy playing in the rain. If you mentioned the summer graduation parties, Fred would lead into a twenty-minute diatribe on how Billy played soccer with all his cousins at their graduation parties and won every game. It was non-stop gloating with Fred. Once the season started, I made a point to avoid him at all costs.

Fred, of course, wasn't the only odd person I met while involved with soccer. There was Mrs. Stonehart, whose alien like neck always seemed to lengthen around open doors giving you what Jeff Hopper called, that "ET look", who threatened to quit her son's team unless the club changed the color of the uniforms. Then there were the Morils, who punctuated many of their comments with, "let's do what's best for the kids," but had no problem skimming money from the concessions they ran at the tournament fund-raising tent every year, and of course, the Hendricks, who composed and read the Invocation at the Club banquet, yet would show up two hours before the outdoor games to start a "parking lot" party, sneaking double shots of rum into their coke cans until they were rocked from drinking so much they would bark a litany of profanities at the referee, and Akinori Nakata, the very respectful and bowing Japanese automotive executive, who made a pass at Mrs. Longertonge, a team mom who wrote in her restraining order, "Mr. Nakata kept insisting I be an "indiscreet American woman," and there was Benny Speeres, a dim-witted rough carpenter, who was always unemployed, who couldn't resist telling everybody at Club events that his two kids were the best players in the history of the Crusaders, and Constance Fallmouth, who was a middle aged and married team manager, who had meth-lab eyes on a tired and worn out face, who liked to wear her pants so snug it would bedevil the young novice coaches into following her around like sleep-walking Casanovas.

At times, the coaches weren't any better. We had a couple of young metro-sexual types we nick-named the "vaggie twins"—"puss and wuss" on account of both men placing a lot of importance on their appearance, making sure their hair was always coifed and they were properly attired in their tight fitting Adidas wear. Both men took themselves too seriously, since, as they often pointed out in the coaching meetings, they were the highest certified coaches in the state of Michigan. Though both men played at a low second division college level, neither of the men would acknowledge Bobo whenever he was in the room, even though, only a few decades earlier, Bobo played in a World Cup and was considered to be one of the world's greatest midfielders.

My personal favorite member of the staff was Johnny Hollifield, a short stocky hard drinking pot smoking ladies man, who loved feeling the stringy hairs of his graying mullet float in the air whenever he walked onto the field. Johnny always coached the "C" teams, aspiring never to get better—only seeking a number of teams so he could collect a number of paychecks and phone numbers from separated or unhappy mothers. Johnny told me once, while we sat in the game room at the Club's indoor training center, "Any kid whose mother has a great ass makes my team—automatically!"

It was in that very same conversation with Hollifield, I learned about another coach—a coach with a considerable history, a coach whose behavior was so crude, so unconscionable, and so unethical, he couldn't get a risk management card from the sanctioning boards, disallowing him to coach youth players from the sidelines.

His name was Sonny Christopher. From what Johnny told me, Sonny had spent five years in a Louisiana prison for beating his pregnant girlfriend to near death. That was just one crime in a lifetime of brutal attacks that took over three pages in the official police records. When Christopher couldn't find any coaching jobs down in the south, he moved back north to live with his mother. The word out on the street was that he was hooking up with the Raiders to be a team trainer in the very age Bobo and I coached in.

Johnny Hollifield told me he had roomed with Sonny Christopher twenty years earlier, when they had been freshmen on the soccer team at Macomb University, a small Division II school north of Detroit.

"He had a list on everybody," Johnny added.

"What do you mean a list?"

"Any person he believed had wronged him; got their name put in his notebook of his, and then he makes it his life long mission to get even with that person."

"He told you that?"

"I saw his book."

Johnny went on to tell me about Christopher's checkered past, how his alcoholic father used to beat him and his brothers on a daily basis, how his mother left the father once to live with her mother and father and how the husband bloodied them all up and dragged his wife by the hair into his car and drove her back home.

"He told you all this?" I repeated, not quite ready to believe it.

"Yeah—he opened up to me one time, I don't know why. I'm scared too death of the guy" Johnny replied.

According to Johnny, Christopher hated to lose. He took it personally if another team beat his. He would go so far as to even intimidate the opposing coach physically—on or off the field.

"I know one guy he really hates," Johnny offered as he picked up his team rosters he had been filling out while we spoke.

"Who's that?"

"Bobo."

"Why?"

"Don't ask me. Ask Bobo."

* * *

To be honest, I didn't rush to Bobo to find out what was between him and Sonny Christopher. At the time, I had other problems, like what was going on at work with Santos Garcia, a Mexican national driver of ours.

Santos's nickname was "lover boy." A wife and a family of nine kids did not keep the long-haul driver from attempting to score with as many of the ladies as he could.

Frankie warned him many times at the terminal, in front of me, my uncles, mechanics, and other staff, that a "warm pussy," would be Santos's downfall. I distinctly remember Frankie looking Santos right in the eye after one lecture, making sure Santos understood, "that no warm pussy better be the downfall of Frankie." Then Frankie repeated to everybody a phrase we heard him speak a million times. "We fly under the radar."

Santos was not accustomed to being spoken to in that way. A weightlifter at six-feet-two and 195 pounds, his presence filled a room as he walked into it. Even the men, who worked for my father, gave Santos a quiet respect.

There is a border crossing in Del Rio, Texas, a newer customs facility about two hundred miles northwest of Laredo, Texas. On a Friday night, I received a phone call from my night dispatcher sometime around 7 pm. He told me that Santos was being held at the border for trying to smuggle a fourteen year old Mexican girl into the United States by hiding her under the mattress in his sleeper. Fortunately, since the automotive load Santos was carrying had an extremely tight deadline, there had been no time to combine his legal cargo with contraband.

I broke the news to Frankie at his house. I told him our tractor was seized in Del Rio and that Santos was sitting in the local jail pending charges. Frankie placed his enormous hand in his mouth and bit it. Loud Sicilian words, the tone of which could be understood in many languages, spewed out, loud enough to wake up my mother who had been sleeping in her blue room. Frankie tugged my arm and dragged me down to his office in the basement.

He yanked the phone to his ear and called my uncles, then called his legal advisors. Within a half-hour, they all joined us in the basement, some skittishly pacing while Frankie made violent threats on Santos's life.

Frankie pointed to "Uptown" Eddie Hazleton, his upscale attorney, who specialized in laundering money.

"Get on the next flight to Del Rio. Let that

motherfucker know if he says one word I'm gonna kill every person in his family, every whore he's ever fucked, every aunt and uncle…

I stood up and made a timeout gesture. "I'm out of here," I mumbled, fixing my pants that were clinging to my legs.

Frankie nodded. I kissed my uncles on their cheeks. "Take care of your mother," Frankie said to me as I neared the stairs.

When I reached the kitchen, I was met by my mother, who had a pensive look on her face. "What happened?," She realized something was going on with so many sudden visitors.

"We had an accident mom," I told her, quickly lying to cover for my father.

"An accident? Was it bad?"

"It wasn't good. It was a roll-over down in Kentucky. Thank God nobody was hurt."

I put my arms around my mother and hugged her. It felt so good to have her hug me back with so much tenderness. For a second or two, I felt like I was a little boy again.

"Have you had any more visits from your friend the ghost?" I asked her, being pro-active, knowing eventually she would bring it up.

Mother pulled away from me without a reply other than, "Thank you for asking sweetie."

"Well?"

"He came to me the other night. He told me your sister was in a wonderful place."

CHAPTER 8

A T THE TIME, I had no idea what happened to Santos. I know we took care of his bail—I saw the receipt on my father's desk, about a week after Eddie Hazelton and my Uncle Angelo returned from the Texas border.

After another week, I started receiving phone calls at the office from Santos's wife Maria. Due to the language barrier, Roberto Gonzalez, our bi-lingual operations manager, translated the conversation for me.

"She says she hasn't seen a check in two weeks from Santos."

"Tell her we'll send her some money." Roberto nodded, and then spoke Spanish into the phone.

"She is running out of food. She can only survive for another day or so."

"Tell her I will wire money to her right now."

When I confronted my father in his office about

Santos he agreed we should send Santos's wife a good chunk of money.

"Send her 5K," he told me. "I don't want those kids going hungry."

When I asked Frankie where Santos was he looked at me and shrugged.

"I wish I knew," he said. "I want to get that bastard. This could cost us a lot of money."

Frankie seemed sincere when he spoke to me. He didn't look away like he usually did when he lied.

"You mean he's hiding out on us?"

"He knows he's in trouble. Sooner or later I'll find him."

"What are you going to do with him?"

My father snapped. "What am I going to do? What am I going to do? Maybe I'll have tea with him and the Queen to discuss his driving etiquette. What the fuck!" Then my father pointed at me. "Remember our deal. Stay the fuck out of my side of the business."

* * *

It was Good Friday, at the Veneration of the Cross, when I first saw Sally Livingston. Her husband James and their two teenage boys and young daughter stood at the foot of the altar, behind a huge wooden crucifix, holding it upright at an angle with a group of five more men and women.

Although I had never met Sally, I felt ill at ease as

I approached the large crucifix, for it seemed as I got nearer, Sally's eyes peeped out at me from beneath the beam of the cross, and were glued to mine as I walked in procession.

For a moment, I felt dizzy and nauseous, a warmth of anxiety surged through me, to the point I started to sweat, and when my right leg buckled a little, I felt an overwhelming urge to bolt from the line.

The afternoon sun streaked through the windows at the top of St. John Vianney. The altar chalice glimmered, casting a gold tint across the room, washing the faces of all who stood in line in a bright yellowish hue.

Convinced the dizziness was making my mind play tricks on me, another giant crucifix, cloaked in purple and attached to the wall high above and behind the altar, seemed to lunge forward, appearing closer and more stark, jerking and dilating right above the heads of Sally and her family.

Though I was supposed to pray when I returned to my pew, my mind raced trying to place where I had seen her youngest son. His face looked familiar to me. I whispered to Jenny and she whispered to Luca asking if he knew who the boy was. Luca whispered back that the boy had played against us at the Total Soccer indoor arena in Fraser. He played for a small club called North Macomb. Jenny smiled and gave a look like she remembered.

"He was the one who scored all the goals against us,"

she quietly revealed to me, barely audible.

Normally, I wait for people to introduce themselves to me. I surprised Jenny when I introduced myself in the church foyer to both Sally and her husband James. Sally responded as if she knew all about me.

"You're the coach of that super great team called the Crusaders."

"I help out."

"Danny prays every night he'll have a chance to play for your team some day. He knows his team stinks."

"Why didn't you come to our tryout?"

"Your club costs too much money for us right now. James was laid off for almost six months. The Michigan economy isn't the greatest."

James, who had the wimpiest handshake I ever had the misfortune of clutching, nodded his head in agreement. He seemed like a guy who wanted not to be seen, a guy who was so uncomfortable with small talk he would prefer to hide behind a beam. When it came to talking, Sally was the opposite of her husband, but she shared a similar look her husband had, an uppity pious appearance, a distinct facial quality often seen on the faces of the Pilgrims in a painting I recalled seeing in my youth. When Sally told us her children were home schooled, that explained everything to me. Those damn home schoolers I thought. They all have that same look.

Sally's skin had a pasty opaqueness to it and she wore her brown hair short in an unattractive Dutch cut. She was built diminutively, with a healthy set of breasts for her size, and seemed to be in good shape for a mother of three, who, by my guess, was somewhere in her mid thirties. Though she was thin, her tan pants were loose on her backside, revealing to me in my mind what looked like air pockets trapped in the key places of her figure.

Once Sally and Jenny started talking, I knew I wouldn't have the opportunity to speak. James sort of drifted away so I introduced Luca to Danny, who was a good foot taller than Luca, and was already getting a thin mustache.

"You're the kid with the best moves I've ever seen," said Danny to Luca.

"And you're as fast as lightning," Luca responded.

An idea popped in my head about an upcoming tournament we were playing in. Why not invite Danny to the National Soccer Ranking Cup tournament in Illinois as a guest player? When I asked Sally about Danny playing for us in the tournament she didn't hesitate.

"That's a great idea," she said to both Jenny and me. "This way Danny can get to know the boys so by the next tryout, with God's help, hopefully we'll have enough money to come to the team full-time."

After we exchanged phone numbers, and said our goodbyes, Jenny needled me about the real reason we're supposed to go to church.

* * *

On the Friday before the tournament, I picked Bobo up in my red Ford 150 pick up truck around 3 p.m. With Luca and his teammate Pepe in the back seat playing their video games, Bobo and I settled in our seats for the five hour drive to Chicago. Jenny couldn't make this trip as her mother was coming into town from Vermont. The two had planned the little vacation almost a year earlier. When I kissed her goodbye, Jenny teared up.

"I'm gonna miss you guys," she said.

"You've got your mother coming in," I reminded her.

Jenny rolled her eyes. Her lip quivered, her eyes were pooling up, indicating she was about to burst into tears. I quickly hugged her to settle her down.

"It could be worse," I told her, pulling her close to me.

"What could be worse?" she asked.

"What if it was my mother you were spending the weekend with?" I got her to laugh.

"You got me there."

* * *

During the drive, Bobo told me one story after another. He was wired up, and I could only guess that his brother and neighbors were all on vacation leaving Bobo unable to speak to anyone for awhile, for when he clicked on his seatbelt he was ready for company so he unleashed one story after another. Some of the stories he told me twice, or I had heard them before in previous conversations we'd had. It didn't matter. I wasn't going to be rude.

Feeling comfortable enough in the car as we spoke, I asked him why he chose to leave Bulgaria. I also asked why he had chosen to leave his family behind to start a new life.

"I had no choice. Soccer not fun anymore. Had to play just to live," he answered simply. "I was like a slave, playing soccer for my masters."

Bobo went on to explain the mood of his country at the time, how, in the shadow of the Soviet Union, communism spread to Bulgaria, and what it did to destroy the hopes and dreams of the people. He told me during his last year there; he and his brother Jordan were under constant surveillance, twenty-four hours per day. Even before he considered defecting, the government had armed guards watching Jordan and his brother's room at all times. The communists worried most about their best players defecting. They knew the Americans would try to lure their talented players away with offers they couldn't compete with.

"We play in Spain and I had to get permission to go to the bathroom," Bobo told me, causing me to glance at him while I was driving. Growing more curious about his situation, I looked at him and asked, "If you and your brother were being watched so closely, how did the two of you get on the train the day? What crime had you committed?"

"Mario," he said, tapping my driving arm to get my attention again.

"We had already been caught trying to escape. An informant turned us in. The train was taking us back to our trial or to our death."

Realizing that Luca and Pepe were listening in on the conversation, the car became uncomfortably quiet for a few minutes or so. Then Bobo clutched my arm again.

"Mario?"

"Yes, Bobo?"

"The guard could have easily killed my brodder and me."

Looking puzzled, I turned and did a double take at Bobo. "Now, I'm more confused Bobo."

"Like any soldier, he was a trained marksman. Could have killed us easily. He wanted us to live—wanted us to be free."

"How do you know? Did he whisper that to you and Jordan?"

"No. It was in his eyes. I have dreamt of those eyes for twenty years. Believe me when I tell you, it was written in his eyes."

The Michigan cornfields skirted my periphery as we drove past row after row. After another considerable pause, I changed the subject back to the team. Bobo's enthusiasm returned. The team had worked hard and he was looking forward to being tested at the NSR Cup in Naperville, Illinois. Along with the best teams in the Midwest and the East coast, the Raiders would be there, giving us an opportunity to play them in the semi-finals if we both made it through pool play.

Close to Battle Creek, just after Luca and Pepe asked if we could stop at the next fast-food spot, a white SUV sped by going ninety, beeping the horn continuously, and nearly side swiping us. When I turned my head toward the car, a man's hand was raised above the top of the vehicle, giving us the finger. I turned to Bobo.

"That looked like Sonny Christopher," he said to me.

"You recognized him?"

"I recognize him anywhere."

"You two don't like each other?"

"Mario. I never have a conversation with the man. He hates me because his teams never beat me once."

"He has never beaten you?"

"No. he is 0 and 7."

I could feel my Sicilian blood starting to boil, thinking about how close Christopher came to hitting the truck.

"I'll tell you one thing Bobo," I said, as I adjusted myself in my seat again.

"What's that Mario?"

"He's fuckin with the wrong guy."

* * *

In the hotel lobby, I introduced Sally Livingston to the parents on the team. When Sally learned that Bobo and I needed to check the team in at another hotel, where the tournament headquarters were, she suggested letting Luca and Pepe hang out with her and Danny. For a man, that was an easy decision to make.

At the Marriott, Fred Castil was already waiting in line for our respective age group. Knowing Bobo drank a lot of coffee; I went over to the hospitality table and poured Bobo and myself a cup.

Bobo positioned himself on the arm rest of a leather lobby couch. I stood next to him, looking above the madness of the crowd. The individual words of chatter were lost in the sounds of the hotel's four story waterfall. It was interesting watching the coaches and team managers hustling and buzzing around, from one table to the next, flipping through page after page of tournament regulations in front of officious and faceless tournament coordinators.

Out of the corner of my eye, I saw a man lean over the second story railing and heard him say,

"Is that you Bobo?" I looked at Bobo, then the man. Bobo smiled and waved.

"Sentilli. Peter Sentilli, how you doing?" asked Bobo.

Peter Sentilli pointed at Bobo in a demanding way.

"Bobo, don't move. I'm bringing my wife and kids down."

Curiously, I approached Bobo.

"Who's that?"

"That's Peter. He play on my first team. Good player. Made it on to the national team and played in Europe—second division."

"You're kidding me?"

The elevator opened and Peter, a man in his early thirties, ran to Bobo like a long lost son. He held Bobo tight for minutes, a long enough period of time I knew Bobo was getting uncomfortable with. I could see Bobo's face on Peter's shoulder. Bobo repeatedly tapped Peter's back with his right hand.

"It's OK, it's OK" Bobo kept saying to him.

When Peter turned, it was clear he was overcome with emotion. He grabbed his wife's hand and brought her over to Bobo's side.

"Honey—this is the man I've told you about all these years. This is the legend. This is Bobo."

Honestly, I can't recall crying ever in my adult life. For a moment, I felt a lump in my throat so foreign to me, that in order to avoid embarrassment, I walked away to get another cup of coffee.

We moved to a cafeteria table in the corner and settled into the seats. Bobo introduced me as his new friend, his savior he called me, the man who revived his coaching career, the man who let Bobo do his job, to coach and train the boys without any politics. Bobo told Peter it was the first time in a long time that he simply could concentrate on what he believed God's purpose for him on earth was.

"I am here to teach children how to play the most beautiful game in the world correctly. It is my destiny," he announced to all of us.

At the table, Peter told one story after another about Bobo in the early years. In Peter's words, Bobo could not speak a word of English the first time they met. Peter and his friends had seen Bobo day after day at Heritage Park in Ann Arbor, Michigan. They called him the man from the circus—for each day, always at the same time, Bobo put on an elaborate show with the soccer ball for all the kids at the playground. He juggled the ball with his feet while standing, and then maintained the juggling when he sat down. Once he stood up, with either heel, he would rainbow the ball high over his head, catching the ball and settling it in the crest of his neck. Then he popped it up high again so he could catch and hold it gently on the top of his shoe.

The boys were eager to learn the game of soccer. They started playing daily with Bobo, grasping the fundamentals by watching every move Bobo made.

"The ball did all the talking," said Bobo, taking another sip of coffee from his styro-foam cup, with a little grin at the side of his mouth.

"Soon," Peter told me, "we were playing two to three hour scrimmages with Bobo. Our parents thought we were at the park playing baseball. Hell, the only thing we were using our mitts for was to form the goals."

One of the boy's fathers eventually found out about the free soccer lessons Bobo was giving out. Through a local Bulgarian, who worked in an appliance repair shop, the father was able to speak to Bobo about creating an organized team in a league. Bobo agreed to train the team and from which, three players emerged as national players.

Peter was at the tournament for his youngest daughter, who was playing in the eight and under division. He lived in Indiana, near Terre Haute, the part of the State they call Larry Bird country.

"I hope you know what a treasure you have there," Peter said to me, tipping his cup like a toast in my direction.

"My son Luca loves him."

"He made the game so much fun for me. Every day was like living a dream."

"Did he ever use this expression? Someday you'll play for 50 million?"

Peter almost choked on his coffee.

"Through the translator, he told me that a million times. I only made a fraction of that while in Europe."

"What about the St. John story?"

There was stillness. Peter shook his head with a dumbfounded look on his face.

"I don't remember any story about St. John. What's that about?"

We both looked at Bobo. Bobo put his cup down. As if he was our father, he stood between us in his shiny Real Madrid jersey and placed his arms on both our shoulders.

"Mario, Peter. That story only for Luca—who is Mario's son. He's a special player—very rare midfielder."

Bobo turned toward Peter and slanted his head.

"Peter. Luca like Zidane and Beckham all in one body."

Peter's face lit up.

"I've got to come see your son play. Coming out of Bobo's mouth, your kid must be some kind of sensation."

Before we left each other, he asked us for the time and the field location for our next game. He told us he would try to get a few of the national staff members to watch the game.

CHAPTER 9

WHAT A NIGHT. When I got back to the Radisson, Sally told me the boys were already asleep in her room.

"They crashed early after playing video games. I'll have them down in time for the morning run."

I don't know if it was the self brewed beer Fred had given me when I passed by his room, or because I was sleeping alone, or if it was the comments Bobo and Peter Sentilli had made about Luca before I left the other hotel, but I dropped around midnight like a ton of rocks and fell into one of the most beautiful deep sleeps I can ever remember.

I started having these incredible dreams, dreams that were crisp, vivid, and radiant, different in size and color from my normal dreams, like the difference between watching a movie on a television set versus a large screen at the theater.

I kept seeing an elevator open and close, open

and close, with a boy running out into Bobo's open arms. That's got to be Peter I thought to myself while dreaming, holding a running conversation with myself as the images flashed between my unconscious and subconscious mind. No. No. It wasn't Peter—it looked more like Bobo's son, the son in the photo on Bobo's mirror in his living room.

Then I could see my father and my uncles, not as older men, not with their double chins and puffy faces, but like in my favorite photo of them, when I was real young, when times were innocent—the three of them positioned at the table in their white t-shirts, fat Angelo up from his chair with his arm around Frankie, while Tony, with his toothy grin, made rabbit ears behind my father's head. Frankie, for some reason, had his thumbs together, as if he was making a field goal post out of his hands for someone on the other side of the table who was ready to launch a paper football. I love that photo I told myself.

Then a man appeared in my dreams, a man I had never seen before. Could it be Radek, the Polish ghost my mother spoke of, as he kept coming in and out and turning his hands in a way a game show host on TV presents a prize? Then I saw Sofie, at twelve, in her training suit she always wore for my fights sitting in my room, the room I want to live in, the room in heaven I wanted to live forever in. She started posing on my couch that sits in front of the fireplace, making funny faces at me, while the texture of the dream film became scratchier and fainter. She is in a beautiful place I told myself, she is in a beautiful place, and I never felt such happiness, such ecstasy.

Then out of nowhere, the way men's dreams often begin and finish, the dream jumped to a scene with an old girlfriend. I saw Tina, in her yellow bikini, her voluptuous ass wiggling across her backyard right in front of me, in slow motion, and then back, in super slow motion, and then, soon as I felt a warmth in my loins, I heard a thump, a thump loud enough to awaken me—loud enough to get me to sit up in the bed—up in the swarthy dull blueness of the room.

Who had any idea what Sally Livingston was planning. Who knew that in the middle of the night, she would leave her room, go to the front desk, pretend like she lost her hotel key, give the receptionist my room number, and then slip into my room at the very moment I'm most vulnerable, strip all her clothes away and stand naked in the darkness until my eyes adjusted and could see her outline at my bedside, her eyes aching for me to take her into my arms.

It could have been any woman. When I pulled her to me, the sheet spun around us, billowing out like the skirt of a whirling dervish. I pressed her deep into my mattress—my loins so sexually overcharged I was afraid I would hurt her with the thrusts but she urged for more while she kept kissing, biting, and clawing me. I turned her around and we fell in between the bed, the sheet still swathed around us—she pressed her hand against the wall while I came in from behind her. She turned her neck easily with her eyes closed and opened her mouth for a second, just enough to let out a wild moan.

She was a caged animal. Sally's tongue pushed up and down and rolled like hanging sponges at the car wash, moving everywhere across me, restlessly exploring every inch of skin I knew to have. Finally, I couldn't take it anymore. I lifted all one hundred pounds of her and took her into the shower where she laughed like a little girl in my arms and told me, right before I turned her sideways to walk across the threshold of the bathroom floor,

"I've been waiting fifteen years to have a man make love to me like that."

At around 4 a.m., she tip-toed out of my room, and I, not yet aware of my transgressions, dropped back exhausted on to the bed—face first.

When I was awakened, though the day appeared to be a little overcast, I elected to wear my sunglasses. Inside my mind, the way I felt about myself, I wanted to hide my entire face when I went down to the hotel restaurant. Sally was there with all the other mothers, buttering their sons toast or pouring milk into their cereal bowls. Sally winked at me, letting me know she was very happy about what had happened a few hours earlier. I squeezed in next to Luca at the booth, kissing his head as he forked his scrambled eggs and sausage.

The first day went as planned. We beat up on the Chicago Magic team easily 4-0 in the first game. Luca, Pepe, Danny, and the other boys put on quite a performance, moving the ball around the field with ease, slotting through-balls in between the startled Magic defenders at will. Coach Mahovolich, who was the director of the entire Chicago Magic program, approached Bobo after the game and asked about Luca and Danny. Mahovolich explained to Bobo that he was the regional olympic development head coach. He was interested in seeing Luca and Danny at the next ODP camp.

In the second game, Mt. Carmel United, the previous season's champion, did not answer the bell against us. We scored in the first minute, when Luca played a heel pass to Pepe, who blew by the unsuspecting defender and finished his shot. The game ended up 3-1. The Mt. Carmel goal came off a corner kick—a beautiful header redirected by a Mt. Carmel defender who seemed to have jumped ten feet in the air. Bobo was so impressed with the effort of the boy who scored; he gave him the game ball after the whistle blew.

When we returned to the hotel, the team parents decided they were going to order pizzas and have a party by the pool. Every one had a few hours to kill so a few of the mothers decided to shop at the mall nearby while some of the fathers went looking for the nearest golf course so they could play a quick nine. All I wanted was to nap. Luca was tired as well. We chilled out in our room, sleeping for awhile, and then watched hi-lights on ESPN of Tiger Wood's latest round.

Luca called Jenny to tell her how well he was doing. When I got on the phone, Jenny sounded so excited—she told me she wished she could take the next flight out to Chicago to be with us.

"Bring your mother," I told her.

"Very funny. You know she hates sports."

"How can you hate sports? It's what we live for."

"It's what guys live for."

Jenny ended the phone conversation with a bunch of mushy girl chatter. I told her I would call her right after the championship game.

* * *

At the pool, when Sally Livingston walked in wearing her two piece bathing suit, Fred nudged me and said, "Your girl looks pretty good."

I pushed him back, half angry and half paranoid. "Whaddaya mean my girl?"

Fred looked at me a little perplexed. "You know, you brought her to the team."

I thought to myself, what a dork Fred was. "Choose your words better Fred," I said to him, feeling a little flush as if everybody on the team knew about our rendezvous.

Sally did look pretty good. When she went to the mall, she had her hair cut differently—shorter with a cosmopolitan look. Wearing more make-up as well, her cheekbones seemed to be accentuated, and her eyes, now outlined with mascara, gave her a certain Cleopatra look that filled her face with raw sexuality.

Twenty minutes later, while everybody on the team filled their faces with pizza, Sally was on top of me in my room, grinding her hips into me, moaning so loud I had to warn her to quiet down. "But I've never been with a man like you," she cooed into my ear. "So strong, so muscular—I want to be with you forever."

I couldn't help myself. I was shamefully impassioned by her advances. In my mind, I justified my actions, blaming them on my Sicilian heritage, something my father and uncles always did. One of fat Angelo's favorite expressions around the office was, "There's nothing sadder than an unused erection."

All the men I knew in the family had mistresses. In our culture, it was a right of passage, something every man had to do at least once before he died.

We won our last game in pool play the next morning by a 4-0 score. When the Raiders squeaked out a tie against their opponent, because they scored more goals in the tournament, they were able to advance through their bracket to play us in the semis.

Andy Mayer had to coach the game since Sonny Christopher wasn't allowed to be on the side-line. Bobo didn't look a bit worried before the game. He warmed up the team with their same pre-game ritual, and then took the boys in the corner to talk to them.

"Boys. This will be easy game," Bobo said. "Why?"

Danny put up his hand first. Bobo pointed to him.

"Cause they don't pass?"

"Not bad. Good answer... but not complete story." Bobo slowly bent down to look at the boys at eye level.

"The Raiders play like theees. Stud on top. Stud in the back. Keeeck balls up to stud and he try to score. They put two gorillas in the middle to win balls, not to set anything up."

The boys and I chuckled at the sight of Bobo's impression of a gorilla.

"The Raiders will never put three passes together. Never! All you have to do is possess the ball, make them chase you, then look for their weakness and attack it. Be calm. Be smart. Be ready."

The boys jumped up. They put their hands together in a huddle and sprinted onto the field. When the ball was touched by the Raider striker to begin the game, the game from that point was ours. The Raiders were never really in it. By marking their striker with Alex Pearhardt, and leaving our sweeper ten yards behind them, our team essentially took their best player out of the game. I don't recall the boy ever getting a shot off.

On the offensive side, since we maintained possession of the ball for over seventy-five percent of the game, it was a simple matter of time before the Raider players tired from chasing our boys.

Bobo told me after our first goal. "Playing defense whole game is very taxing." He had to repeat the word taxing to me a couple of times for with his thick accent; I could not understand what he was saying. "Mario. Now that first goal is scored, the floodgates will be open."

He was right. We scored four goals in a ten minute span before half-time. Bobo took our kids at the half to sit under a tree. I watched Andy Mayer take the Raider boys to where Sonny Christopher was standing at the eighteen yard line of their goal. Christopher would not let the boys sit. I heard him tell the boys they deserved to be standing in the hot sun, they were playing like losers, playing like a team who came to a tournament to prove they could quit. He berated their starting eleven for ten minutes, while Andy Mayer drank water from a trainer's bottle and listened.

The game ended up 7-2 in our favor. The Raider boys left the field without shaking our hands. I watched Sonny Christopher storm off the bleachers and head toward the parking lot. With Andy Mayer beckoning the Raiders back in attempt to get them to be good sports, the boys on the Raider team ignored him and followed Christopher toward the cars.

The final game was a little tougher. Though we won

it easily from a possession stand point, the final score, 2 to 0, was not indicative of our dominance. We couldn't finish our shots, missing easy attempts over and over again. All our opponent's chances came from free kicks or corners, something we needed to work harder on in order to defend. The team we beat was called FC Delco—they were from a highly respected Club out of the Philadelphia area and the reigning State champs from Pennsylvania.

I enjoyed that game so much. With the stress of our rivalry with the Raiders out of the way, I was able for the first time to watch Luca play and allow the match to be fun. I was able to smell the kettle corn sweetening up the air above the tournament grounds, watch the little kids line up gleefully at the snow-cone counter, then watch them peek into the white trophy tent with their lip stained mustaches to catch a glimpse of the giant golden trophies glinting on the tables, awaiting the first and second place teams.

For as far as I could see, the green fields were littered in a festival of color, the uniforms of teams visiting from all over the country, massaging my eyes in oranges with navy, reds together with royal blue, forest greens with gold trim, and purple accented with white and black to name a few.

A little girl blew soap bubbles as her bosomy mother pushed her in a stroller between two adjacent fields. An old heavy set man with a slight limp and lumps of varicose veins cheesing up his legs from his white socks, dropped his freshly garnished hot dog when it slipped from his bun like shower soap from your hands and plopped in the sandy dirt in front of the stand, lifting a plume of dust that dissipated about waist high.

After snapping the top of a Coke can open, I watched three teenage boys wearing yellow tournament marshal shirts stick their thumbs out like hitchhikers when a friend of theirs whizzed by them in a tournament golf cart.

Fighting the fizz after gulping the cola, the carbonation crept back up and fiercely jolted out of me in a rather loud and rambunctious burp. A little embarrassed, and thankful I wasn't close to anybody but Bobo and the boys on the sideline, I scanned my eyes from field to field, listening to the coaches scream, "Send it, Send it!" above the clatter of the crowd.

The Illinois sun was merciless at the peak of the afternoon. In the fields nearby, the corn stood tall yet did not sway a bit in the torturous heat. I rubbed the cold aluminum can against my face until it numbed my skin and beads of condensation trickled down my face. As I bent to sit on top of our team cooler, I noticed, as I carefully listened, that the referee whistles blew incessantly and at different pitches, sounding as dissimilar as the calls of birds perched in the trees lining the park. After shooing a yellow legged grasshopper away, from a distance, I heard the jingle of an ice cream truck approaching and watched head after head turn automatically, (including a ten to eleven year old girl about to take a penalty shot on a field kitty-corner from ours), in the direction of the oncoming music.

Like a kid watching a kite rise and sink in the open sky for hours, I was so enraptured by the joy of my surroundings; I didn't even hear the final whistle to our game blow.

After the game, amidst the chaos of handshakes, hugs, and photos, I felt first, and then noticed in the corner of my eye, somebody with his hands folded, staring at me from a distance of twenty yards or so. When I casually turned and looked over to right side, I could see it was Sonny Christopher, who looked like a gun slinger wanting to draw.

Jeff Hopper, the Club President, always made me laugh by teasing me about my rugged jaw line and my Italian wing tip shoes I always wore. He called me Rockford after the TV character and I, not allowing him to one up me, referred to him, on account of his sandy hair and boyish looks as the "surfer boy" or "Peter Frampton"—the bubble gum rock star of the seventies.

My jaw line was nothing compared with Christopher's. He looked like he was cut out of Mt. Rushmore. With a shaved head and a fu-man-chu tightly cropped on a face that always looked menacing, I could see how the guy intimidated a lot of the local parents and coaching staffs.

What he didn't understand, what he miscalculated with me was my past as a boxer and a fighter. I had fought a thousand times before I ever set eyes on him—I knew the game, knew the stare down routine, knew it from being face to face with my opponent where you smell his breath and his sweat and can hear his heart beat as he peers into your eyes, hoping to find a weakness, challenging your every nerve before you even throw the first blow.

I was younger and bigger than Christopher. I too folded my arms and stared back at him, stared at him in a way no man had ever done, stared at him with a look my father had taught me in the ring, what he called the "death wish look", a look that penetrated into the deepest regions of another man's soul.

In the eighth minute or so, in a flutter of his eye only my trained eye could catch, Christopher acquiesced, and I knew he knew, he was no match for me in a fist fight. If there were going to be problems between us, he would have to seek other means besides a physical confrontation.

With his shoulders down, Christopher spun away and sunk into the emerging crowd.

CHAPTER 10

I RECEIVED SALLY'S LAST message on my beeper May 2nd, a good month-and-a-half before team tryouts. Though I really wanted her son Danny on the team full time, the other side of my mind, the side that contemplated what was good and right, told me to discontinue the relationship.

For two straight weekends after the Chicago tournament, I did make the mistake of meeting Sally a couple of times, once at a Best Western in downtown Utica and another time at the Marriot in Troy.

She scared me. In the back of my mind, I was a little afraid she might reveal the affair to Jenny, yet I was more afraid of her crazed sexual longings. In a short period of time she became a full throttled nymphomaniac, attempting to unzip me in the elevator at the Marriot, trying to straddle me in my car in the parking lot like we were a couple of teen-agers, using her foot to stroke my crotch under the table while we took a little break to eat in the Hotel restaurant.

Sally simply wore me out. On top of the love making, she wanted to talk, talk about team matters, or soccer community matters, or local soccer Club gossip, in long unwinding conversations. Who had time for that? My Uncle Tony once told me if I were ever to take a mistress, make sure I did it the way all the dagos do.

"Get yourself a knockout blond who can't count to ten," he told me. "You bang him hard and then send em out shopping or to the casino," he added.

In one bedside conversation, I did ask Sally why she was no longer interested in her husband.

"He's too good to me," was her reply.

* * *

It was a bad month. Not a lot seemed to go well. At the office, while my father and Angelo were in Atlantic City with their knockout blonds, I received a frantic call from the translator Roberto Gonzales, who had received a frantic call from Santos's wife.

"They killed him," he shouted over the inter office phone.

"Killed who?" I asked.

"Santos. He's dead. Somebody murdered him and his girlfriend."

"Get in here now!" I ordered.

They found the young girl and Santos in the

morning, after a late night rain, hanging and swaying side by side from a large branch of a willow tree in his home town square.

In front of Roberto, who was a boyhood friend of Santos, all I could do was portray the incident as a random act of violence. I remember Roberto dropping onto my office couch as if he was losing his balance. He shook feverishly for a good five minutes. I poured him a shot of whiskey from my bar which he acknowledged in one quick gulp.

Only Uncle Tony was working. I called him on the two-way radio and asked if I could see him at his office in the mechanic's garage.

"C'mon over kid," he responded.

To get to the house of the living dead, I had to walk past mountains of old tires, rotted out trailers, giant black oil slicks stretching and seeping into dried out tire ruts or pools of muddied water. There was a thick filth to the air, a stench rising like steam from the concrete, blowing hot into my face as I clumsily maneuvered my newly polished wing-tip shoes between chunks of concrete rubble.

Through a side door I slinked in unnoticed, jumped onto a one floor escalator that Angelo had put in due to his weight, and knocked on the half-open-door of my Uncle Tony's office... "C'mon on, c'mon in kid and shut the door," Tony ordered in his raspy baritone.

Only a small desk lamp was on. The room was made

even darker, by the deep brown mahogany paneled walls and the leather chairs and couches of forest green and black. Uncle Tony put a glass with ice on the edge of his desk. He leaned over and casually poured amoretto, which flowed like syrup on top of the rocks of ice.

"Have a drink Mario," he said to me. Uncle Tony settled himself into his large chair.

"What's going on?" I wanted to know.

"With what?"

"Santos was found hanging from a tree in Saltillo."

"So?"

"Uncle Tony, I can't believe what…

"Shut your fuckin mouth right now."

I put my hands out as if I were asking why. Uncle Tony slowly pulled a wrapper off a cigar and lit it.

"Unless you want your Uncle Tony to be found hanging in a tree, I can't talk to you about the family business."

"I'm going to have a difficult time finding drivers out of Saltillo now. That's where we get sixty percent of our Mexican force."

"Let us worry about that."

I stood up and started pacing.

"I feel like I'm trapped Uncle Tony."

"Trapped?" he replied. "Sit down kid. I'll tell you all about being trapped." Uncle Tony closed his mouth until I sat down. "Listen kid. Your papa, Angelo and

I didn't ask for this. We were born into it. We weren't given a choice. That's what trapped means."

I put my right hand over my eyes.

"Some kids are born in Africa to a tribe rampant with AIDS, or some kids are born in villages where civil wars kill or orphan them early, and then others wake up at seven and find out they're the god son of "Black Joe" and their fates are sealed forever."

What could I have said after that? Uncle Tony tossed me a cigar. I tried to catch it but it slipped between my hands and landed on my thigh.

"Remember this kid. Your father loves you so much… he lives to protect you. He sacrifices his eternal life so you can live forever. We know we're doomed to hell."

Uncle Tony punctuated his last sentence with a disturbing stare that lasted for a good two minutes. The room suddenly seemed airless and I had trouble drawing a deep breath.

"Can I go now?"

"One other thing."

"What?"

"Get rid of the girl."

Everything wasn't great with the soccer team either. Another incident, which I received blame for, caused a bit of turmoil within our parental group. I felt the wrath for what had happened though it occurred harmlessly. It involved Bobo and our players during a rain out.

In youth soccer, if lightning is observed by a referee, the players must be taken to the parents' cars for a period of fifteen minutes or so. At this particular game, when the lightning was first seen, it was off in the distance, perhaps fifteen miles away. I asked Bobo if he wanted to sit with me in my car with a few of the boys, who asked their parents in the hustle and bustle of getting off the fields if they could wait out the storm in Luca's car. I had Jenny's full-sized van that day—with a television and video player in the back. The boys on the team loved watching films or playing video games in what they termed, "the Santini mobile." Bobo declined my invitation, telling me if the storm got bad he would sit it out in his own van.

When the storm did hit, it hit hard. The van rocked from the wind while it was impossible to see anything out the front window as the rain lashed against it. I turned the air on to cut the vapor on the inside window, then put the wipers on full blast, hoping to rid the front window from the surge of water flowing across it so I could look through and see the fields.

At first the boys were oblivious to the storm. When a bolt of lightning jolted something nearby, the thunder exploded so loudly the boys huddled against each other.

"Are we gonna die Mr. Santini?," asked Pepe, in mock hysteria.

When there was a pause with the rain. Luca happened to slide a side window open that had a screen in front of it. From the little vent opening, he saw Bobo still sitting on the bench.

"Bobo's still out there," he told the boys. Before I could turn, all five boys were out the door running for Bobo.

"Stay inside," I shouted as they dashed toward the bench. Ignoring my own words, I stepped out of the van and followed them.

"Bobo! Bobo!" the boys screamed in unison, dipping their heads in the hard rain that quickly started up again. Bobo had his shirt off and was wringing it when the boys started calling his name. A kite string of lightning lit up the sky, followed by a fierce and penetrating snap of thunder, startling the boys who dropped to their knees, freezing black silhouettes of the boys in my mind's eye as if a strobe light was flashing on them. All of us ran up to Bobo.

"Get in the van Bobo, get in the van, I yelled above the boys pleas.

I'm OK," said Bobo.

"If you don't get in that van, I'm going to put you over my shoulder and take you there!"

Bobo nodded like he understood.

As we ran toward the van, a few of the parents of the boys shouted from their opened car windows at us for being out in the rain. When the game resumed, two of them, Mrs. Bortano, and Fred's wife, Marriane made sure they gave me a piece of their mind for endangering their children while the storm was in full force.

To make matters worse, later in the month, after a coaching staff meeting, Jeff Hopper invited me to have a beer with him at a local watering hole called the Harkins Pub. With my car filled with uniforms, balls, corner flags, you name it; we decided to hop into Hopper's Vibe. The Pub was no more than a few miles away from our training headquarters.

The Pub has a fairly large parking lot, although not especially well lit. We arrived about dusk—a paint splash of pink and lavender filled the sky. Hopper and I were engaged in a conversation about the advantages of playing a flat back four defensively, when, as Hopper crept slowly through the back end of the lot looking for a parking spot, he suddenly hit the brakes hard, threw the car in park and ordered me to get down. We both slid down in our seats like there was a professional hit coming our way.

"What is it?" I asked.

Hopper snuck his head above the steering wheel to catch a peek. "Take a look Mario. It's your buddy Christopher," he said.

"Why are we hiding from him?" I asked. I started to sit up in my seat.

"Wait. Is that Danny's mother?" asked Hopper. Now I knew why I needed to stay down.

"I thought she was married?" he asked again.

"She is."

"Oh, shit. Mario. Take a look."

Slowly I inched my eyes above the dash. Over to the right, where they couldn't see us, there they were, in full view. Sally Livingston, unaware of us watching her, was being lifted up in her painted on leather pants by Christopher. With his hands on her ass, he pushed her up against a car where he dry humped her for a good five minutes as the two locked their lips like they were trying to eat each others tongues.

"I guess Danny's not trying out for our team," said Hopper sarcastically, chuckling. Not wanting to watch any more, I pointed to the parking lot exit.

"Let's go to Applebees," was all I could think of at the moment.

Hopper shook his head. "It's too bad. She's nothing but his whore now," he told me, as he pulled his Vibe out of the parking lot and on to 21 Mile Road.

CHAPTER 11

JUNE OF THAT year was the greatest month of my life. After Easter, Jenny was despondent about what she perceived as her inability to get pregnant. She had a major melt down—her grief was so deep it caused her to cry in a frenzied way for hours while I tried to console her on the couch in our family room.

Searching for the right answers to give her was not easy. Instead of lecturing her or pacifying her with superficial clichés I opened up to her about my dissatisfaction with her approach on making love only when she was ovulating or near to ovulating.

"Why didn't you just tell me this before,?" she asked, turning her head and staring at me from about three inches away.

"You're scaring me."

"What?"

"You're too close. Your freckles are the size of large moles." Jenny gave me a soft back hand as a love tap.

The ice was broken and we began to talk.

I continued. "I do think I told you—maybe not directly—but you must have known…"

She went on to tell me about how hard she prayed for a child, that she wanted a daughter for me and my family so it could ease the tragic memories of losing my sister.

"When has God ever given you anything immediately after you've prayed for it?" I asked her.

"I've been praying for months—since we decided to have another child."

"What are months? That's nothing in God's time-line."

"When did you become a priest?"

"Smart ass."

We did agree, after talking for hours, that the will of God wasn't something we could alter. If Jenny were to become pregnant, that would be wonderful, and if it didn't happen, we were still a family. Feeling the guilt from my affair with Sally, it was at that point that I decided to put an end to looking at other women, understanding clearly, as we spoke of God, it would be my sins the family would suffer for.

In an ill-attempt to make a point, or to at least stress what I was feeling at that juncture, I told her a story about my boxing days, how nothing ever worked out the way I thought it would. Whenever I thought I was going to whip somebody, or if I thought I was ready to knock another fighter out—something changed, something that would cause the outcome to be different or not as I originally thought it would be. I learned never be too confident, never too sure about myself. It seemed when I least expected something, something good would happen.

How she followed that I'll never know, and perhaps she didn't, and was just being polite, but whatever the case, in the wake of that discussion, we made love, and it was the best love we had made since we were in our early twenties. Some speak about how great "make-up" sex is—well this was post ovulation clinical sanitized go through the motion for six months sex and it was the most passionate I'd experienced with any woman. It was raging yet tender, it was physical yet intimate, and it was selfish yet sincere.

Wouldn't you know, come June 10th, only a couple months from our intense discussion and our new outlook, Jenny rushed into the kitchen while Luca and I were crunching away at our coco-krispies to let us know God had answered our prayers. At last, Jenny was pregnant. Luca and I literally bounced out of our seats and gathered around Jenny for a long and enthusiastic hug. When I called my mother to tell her the good news she started screaming with joy. Frankie grabbed the phone to tell me the celebration would be at their house on Saturday. He was inviting everybody he knew.

"It's too much, it's too much," I told him knowing there was no changing his mind.

What a party Frankie put on. There were more big named dagos at his house than at the wedding of Vito Corleone's daughter. There was Sammy Mancini and his wife, Toots Bommarito the baker, and Judge Vince Saracino, from over at the Federal building in Mt. Clemens. Freddie "the fixer" Antolini, who was a big time bookie, stopped by and so did Eddie Hazleton and another lawyer from his firm. To my surprise, my cousin Stefano was there, who I hadn't seen in ten years, with his wife and twin girls. Even my father's sister, Mary Grace, who he had been estranged for over fifteen years, came to reconcile with him, and give her regards to Jenny and me with our new baby. Aunt Mary Grace held my cheek and tugged on it, "You are my flesh an a my blood," she said in front of the entire crowd.

The only person there who I wished stayed home was a tiny unassuming man named Pasquale Ferrentelli. My cousins told me when I was a kid he was the family's chief assassin. His nickname was "the fog" on account of the fact he was on you before you could even see him. They told me he was a contortionist; he could work his body through any window, through any vent, through any slight opening in the house of his prey. He would wait for his victims for hours, capable of standing motionless for hours in a room, in a closet, behind the curtains—unseen, unheard, almost like he was invisible.

I had nightmares about the guy for years.

But the party raved on. Red wine poured into glasses, champagne corks popped on the hour, old men and woman danced tarantellas in the back yard between games of bocce ball and pinochle. My mother floated on air around the backyard, the front yard, circulating through the house with a glow on her face I hadn't seen in years.

Even Luca joined in the mood of the festivities. While in the kitchen with my father, my uncles, a few second cousins, myself and a few people I didn't know, Luca suddenly blurted out to my father, "Hey Pops, I'm hungry and I need to get to the refrigerator. You think you can stop me?"

That was music to Frankie's ears. Everybody who knew about the challenge cleared to one side of the room. Frankie unbuttoned his shirt as Uncle Angelo brought the gloves in from the laundry room. When Luca pulled his shirt over his head, I was flabbergasted to see light fuzz under his arms. Right under my nose he changed—you could see the cut in his upper frame and a knot in his bicep when he tightened up his gloves.

As if a highly anticipated prize fight was about to begin, the match spread among the guests of the party quickly through word of mouth.

"Frankie's gonna fight again, Frankie's gonna fight again," was broadcasted around the yard, the street, and every room of the house.

My mother stormed into the kitchen expecting to see my father pounding away at one of the guests. Instead, she saw Frankie and Luca in the corner of the kitchen, gloves on, both boxers in their sleeveless t-shirts. She could see old men peeking through the windows and other men elongating their necks from the laundry room to catch a look at the fight.

Luca waved to his grandmother. "I'm gonna make it to that refrigerator this time grandma," he told her. Knowing the two were only playing around, the relief came over my mother's face.

Frankie pushed Luca into the corner and then leaned on him. He started rolling his shoulders into Luca while peppering him with soft rabbit punches. "You gotta counter-punch out of this one kid," Frankie offered as a suggestion. Luca pushed him away, and then teased him with a couple of shots. The crowd rewarded Luca with a little applause. Frankie was pulling his punches, but still, he was in rare form, moving almost seductively around the kitchen, as if he were thirty years younger in his prime. The group gathered in the kitchen was transfixed on his every move, pointing and cheering when he ducked, bobbed, or feigned like he was going to throw a punch.

Luca was able to squirm out of the corner to where he had more room and could dance a little, so of course, he did his version of the Ali-shuffle, and that brought a huge moan of delight from the fans in the kitchen. I was shocked he could pull it off.

Frankie countered by imitating his hero Rocky Marciano, which was the perfect move for the Sicilian "Hit man" in front of all his Sicilian admirers. His imitation was impeccable, even making sure his facial expressions were just like Marciano's. The dagos loved it.

They started chanting, "Rocky, Rocky, Rocky!"

The energy in the room was electrifying—like being at ringside. Luca threw two left handed jabs and an overhand right. Frankie took it right on the chin and played like he was going down, spinning and circling the room like a drunk. Luca, seeing his path open to the refrigerator dashed for it before Frankie could react. Everyone laughed, and then started chanting Frankie's name. Frankie bowed, pulled off his gloves—and then begged for a beer.

Having a little fun of my own, I grabbed Luca and wrestled him down to the floor. Seeing the infamous basket of artificial fruit on top of the dishwasher, I picked up the apple and faked like I was going to throw it at Luca.

"You didn't fight hard enough," I shouted, impersonating my father's voice. As Luca covered up, Frankie slid across the floor on his knees and shielded Luca from any possible blows.

"Never, never," he chortled out. "If anybody ever hurt my grandson, my baby boy, I'll kill him, I'll kill him, I tell you."

Frankie started tickling Luca until Luca, laughing so hard, wriggled his way out of Frankie's grasp. When I turned around, still holding the apple, I could see my Uncle Angelo pointing at me.

"It's time for the Mario show," he said loudly like he was a ring side announcer.

It was my turn. I looked at Frankie. He looked at me and I nodded—his smile beamed with pride. Uncle Angelo and Tony whipped the group up to start chanting my name. "Mario, Mario, Mario!" filled the room. I put on my gloves and put on a show that I know was the best performance of my life. As the bottles of wine were lifted above the men and poured carelessly into their glasses or mouths, I made sure there wasn't a person in that room that didn't get their money's worth.

When I finished, Uncle Angelo took the stage with his bird calls and impressions of Oliver Hardy and Lou Costello. When he started dancing like Chubby Checkers, it was time to take the party back outside, to the patio, to the tent, to the dance floor rented and installed for the special occasion.

* * *

That night, as the party neared its end, my mother grabbed my hand and pulled me down the hallway to her room. Already in the room were Jenny and Luca, who sat next to each other on the right side of the sofa. Jenny blew me a kiss when I walked in. Luca had his hand on her belly like he was gently rubbing it.

"It's time to thank the Lord for your blessing son," said my mother. From a small jewelry box on her book shelf, she pulled out a number of rosaries, all of them different colors, shining like trinkets. She handed each of us one. As my mother sat down on the edge of her sofa, we were startled when Frankie stepped into the room, still in his t-shirt, sweating profusely, and asked,

"Hey, don't I get a rosary?"

I loved that moment. For another hour, I watched my father, the gangster, pray and meditate on the novenas, his aqua rosary getting lost in his giant hand, his voice cracking after saying together with all of us, "Lord hear our prayer," after mother requested in her special intention that our baby be a girl, and that her name be Sofie Marie Santini.

Jenny yawned. Luca was fast asleep with his head comfortably tucked in between the sofa and Jenny's shoulder. Alone in my thoughts, I drifted back to a time when my father would take Sofie and me for our daily visits to see our mother at Glen Eden. We would stand outside her third story window and wait for her to push her hand outside her opened window to wave at us. As kids, it was the only sign we had that mother was still alive.

Most men would have been overwhelmed and crumbled under the circumstances. Outside of receiving a little help from Grandma Clare, who was my mother's mother, Frankie pretty much raised us on our own during those years.

He used boxing to keep us close. He was the manager, I was the boxer, and Sofie was his assistant during those years. Sofie always had my gloves ready, my mouth guard and water bottles packed for every fight. While the fights took place, Pa had Sofie keeping stats, meticulously jotting down how many left jabs I threw, how many overhand rights, how many punches actually connected to the body or face of my opponent.

We were a team, a fighting team. And now in Sofie's room, with my entire family present, and my mind ceaselessly running back into time, I couldn't help but feel overwhelmed by the circumstances of my life.

Deep down, my father, who worked outside the law, was a good man. My mother did the best she could. Sofie was a brother's dream and Jenny and Luca were the loves of my life.

With a new child on the way, with renewed hope for better times ahead, I bowed my head and prayed to the Lord to have mercy on me for my sins and the sins of my family. "Protect me—Protect me from sin Lord," I asked aloud, and added silently to myself, "so no temptation could ever overcome me like the sin of adultery—a sin so grave it could be the cause for ruin of my entire family."

"Make me a better man," I silently repeated, over and over in my mind, as one tiny rosary bead rotated around and between my oily fingers.

CHAPTER 12

A T TRYOUTS FOR that year's state cup, we discovered one player to make up for the loss of Danny Livingston. The boy's name was Adam Jackson, and he was a suburban black boy with a light complexion who had been playing up in an older age bracket. Due to his size, nobody checked to see if Adam was playing in the right age group until Jeff Hopper caught the discrepancy while sifting through the birth certificates one day. Adam was fast, physical, and more tenacious going after the ball than Danny. Bobo was extremely pleased with the pick-up.

"I feel we pick up the last missing piece of the puzzle," were his words to me, as we walked out of the complex together.

"Sometimes God surprises you with a gift."

When we got to the parking lot, we noticed flyers placed under our windshield wipers. As I snatched the paper from my windshield I immediately noticed

Sonny Christopher's photo. Christopher and his cohorts had put together a "cheezy" ad detailing the reasons people in the Rochester Club should transfer to the Raiders. Christopher and his posse must have put the flyers on to all the cars while we were busy on the fields.

For a man just over forty, Christopher operated like an insecure teen-ager, employing tactics that most adults wouldn't consider. One time, he doctored a document with our club logo on it that stated "no blacks" were allowed to play in our club any longer. He nailed the flyers on trees and telephone posts near our home fields at Borden Park. Though the club was proven to be innocent in the matter, Jeff Hopper still had to make an appearance in front of the league commissioner and the board, along with the club attorneys, to prove we were not involved in such a policy. Jeff told me the legal fees to clear the club's name were over $1,000 dollars.

Within a month after tryouts there were other incidents, incidents that were more severe, like the breaking into of our indoor training facility, where the place was trashed and many documents were stolen. Bobo had his tires slashed, while Hopper had a brick thrown through his patio window about 3 a.m. one night, scaring Hopper's wife so much she pleaded for him to give up the club's presidency if Sonny Christopher was behind the attack.

In August, just after we finished two grueling weeks of mini-camps, our front lawn and trees were blanketed with enough toilet paper to fill a parade. My statue of St. Francis of Assisi was knocked down and smashed, leaving the head of St. Francis a good three feet away from his ceramic torso.

There was never any proof of Christopher's involvement; however, the consensus among those of us in the soccer community was Christopher was most likely the guilty party.

At our first coaches meeting of the year, Johnny Hollifield shook his head as Hopper briefed the entire staff on some of the dubious occurrences that had taken place since Christopher had come back into town.

"I told you dudes. I told you. He's gonna get even with every last one of you," said Johnny.

There was no doubt that Christopher's nagging crime spree was taking its toll on me. Deep down, a sentiment was percolating slowly inside the pit of my belly. It was the same feeling I knew as a boxer, a feeling of rage and invincibility, a feeling that could get so severe I was liable to become like my father, where thoughts of committing cruel acts and inflicting punishment or murder to my enemies danced freely and randomly inside my mind. I fought that feeling many times in my life, fought it in the ring, fought it at work, and fought against it within my family, but still, when it was there, there in the ring, that jungle hatred and compulsion to destroy or kill was so strong inside me I literally beat my opponents to death. Only the referee kept things from getting out of control.

On the other hand, I was gripped with guilt, mainly from the brief affair I had with Sally Livingston. I knew if Jenny found out about it that it would hurt her deeply.

Feeling a need deep within me to be cleansed and absolved of breaking one of the Lord's commandments, I checked vicariate bulletins I received after Mass for possible times I could confess my sins. Unlike the days when I was a boy, confession times at the local parishes in the diocese were now, less frequent, and, mainly being offered for an hour in the late afternoon on Saturdays. That was when most of our games were played.

Assuring myself that my intentions were good, I continued through the season, searching in a luke-warm way in between games and road trips to find a Catholic Church and a good priest who would listen to me and help quell the anger lingering inside me.

Week after week went by, with the team winning every game in their league and tournament play, and then in the state cup quarter-finals and semi-finals, until it was time for the eventual show-down everybody in the state had hoped and prayed for. The state cup championship for the under-thirteen age group pitted the two great rivals against each other. It was Bobo's Rochester Crusaders against Christopher's Raiders—the club Fred tagged as the "forces of pure evil."

* * *

It was a beautiful September day for a tournament—a perfect pre-autumn day to continue the University of Michigan versus Notre Dame football rivalry, a game taking place thirty to forty miles to the south west in Ann Arbor, a rivalry of such significant importance, the majority of men around the soccer fields wore ear phones as they wandered around the complex.

A slight wind blew southeast from Saginaw Bay, barely tickling the red corner flags to where they listlessly flickered. Around game time, there was nothing but a scrape of light white clouds filling half the sky over the Saginaw fields. The other half of the sky was all "Carolina" blue, endless to the south as if it was polished tile, reflecting incandescence onto the entire field's living things—illuminating objects to where they glinted and seemed more vivid in my mind.

Before the game, Jenny and the team mothers brought cider and warm doughnuts from the local mill, pouring the cider into small plastic cups while placing the doughnuts on a card table at our side of the field. The scent of cinnamon and apple permeated the sideline, wafting so strongly that even a few parents on the Raiders, those who had casual relationships with a few parents on our team, broke down and asked if they could be included at the table of our feast. I watched Jenny invite them over, her rotund stomach stretching her sweater, an obvious topic of easy discussion among the mothers who could not resist the doughnuts and cider.

The two teams lined up at midfield for the national anthem. When it was finished, both teams waved to their parents and their respective sidelines. The Raiders were in black uniforms with white numbers. The Crusaders wore their all whites with red trim. The two linesmen, with their chests proudly out, ran in their yellow and black pinstripe tops from midfield like a marching band's drum major in opposite directions toward the goals. There they put on a show under the supervision of the center ref as they checked every corner of the netting to make sure it was properly fitted to the goal.

Bobo and Andy Mayer shook hands at midfield as a photo was taken by a league photographer. I watched Sonny Christopher stand up on the top seat of the bleachers across the field and point to his captains the side of the field he preferred them to select if they won the coin toss.

The game started with the Crusaders keeping the ball for the first three minutes of the game. Both teams played with four defenders in the back, playing in a conventional back line with a sweeper ten yards behind their stopper. A misplaced pass from Billy Castil led to a throw in for the Raiders. When they got the ball, it surprised me that they started knocking their passes around pretty well, stealing a page from our play book, as they too tried to posses the ball.

The speed of play for both teams was at a very high level. Luca and Pepe were zipping passes in and out of the midfield, sending passes to the back line or toward the corner flags so the outside midfielders could run on them. Kelleher and Thompson were doing the same for the Raiders, playing very disciplined and smart, though they lacked the touch and creativity of Luca.

The game was scoreless with neither team getting a shot on net until the twenty-sixth minute. Mike Delaney, the Raiders sweeper, burst out of the backfield on a sweeper run once he passed the ball up to Kelleher. Without anyone on our team noticing it except Bobo, the Raiders started storming down the field with an added attacker. Three give and go possessions later; Delaney was on our eighteen with only one player to beat. Delaney cut right and hit a bullet in to the top right corner of the net.

The Raider fans went crazy. One father took the Raider flag and ran it down the entire sideline in front of the Crusader fans. Fred, who normally was a pacifist, tried to wrestle the flag away from the father. A league official had to intercede by taking the flag away from both men.

Two minutes later, Donovan Hermiz, our outside back, played a ball under pressure back to our keeper Aaron Michaels, who took his eye off the ball as he tried to kick it, whiffing it and letting it go right under his foot into the open goal. The stunned crowd went limp watching the ball roll slowly and feebly past the end line. I felt as though someone put a dagger into my back. I watched Luca put his hands on his head in disbelief.

At the half, Bobo didn't speak for the first five minutes of the break. Then he came up with a concocted story that seemed perfect for the moment. He told the boys they were playing with no passion, no purpose after the second goal.

"It's OK," he told them. "If you want to give up, if you prefer to take the second place medals home I can arrange it."

The boys and I looked at Bobo unsure of where he was going in his thinking.

"I have arranged with the league officials, under condition you are too afraid to play second half, to just go over to tent and receive our second place medals now."

"No, no, no," the boys echoed, shaking their heads with a baffled look on their faces.

Bobo pointed to the woods that were at our backs.

"Loook. We could sneak right through those trees on the path there and the parents could meet us on the other side with their cars. Nobody would see us."

"No, no, no," the boys repeated in unison again.

"Then if you want to play, you have thirty minutes left. That's like eternity in soccer. We have lots of time to get back into this game."

I looked at Luca and gave him a "let's turn it on" look. He sprung to his feet.

"Let's go!" he screamed.

The boys ran into a huddle. Bobo put his hand in the middle of all the boy's hands.

"We either go forward or go back home."

The boys broke and the starters ran to the field. Bobo gripped Luca's arm before he could take off.

"I never thought I would say this to you. You are playing too unselfish. Even Mother Theresa gonna try to score if she gets into the box."

First Luca looked at me. Then he looked at Bobo and nodded. It was evident to both of us Luca got the message.

Ten minutes into the second half, Bobo's little talk worked. Luca bent a direct kick from about twenty yards out around the wall and into the upper ninety of the goal. The Crusader side-line had new life. Fred took his coat off with the Crusader logo on it and ran his chubby little body down the sideline. Sonny Christopher ran over to the corner flag to give a piece of his mind to his keeper for being out of position.

After the goal, the Raiders dropped Danny Livingston

back as a fifth defender. When they made that move, Bobo and I knew they were no longer interested in scoring, except with a counter-attack. They were mainly interested in holding the 2-1 lead, a lead they had to keep for about twenty more minutes.

The game became choppy after that. With the Raiders just clearing the ball down the field every time it came to them, the game lost its rhythm. There seemed like there wasn't any room to move on the field, the ball was always in the air, headed back and forth sometimes between teams like a beach ball in the bleachers of a Tiger baseball game.

"Get the ball on the ground," Bobo kept shouting.

Then, with eight minutes to go, right after Bobo told Luca to push up as a third striker, Kelleher blasted a ball forty yards on the fly over the top of our back line where a kid named Newt Nixon picked it up on the second bounce and broke all alone on the goal and beat Michaels to his right for the third Raider goal.

The Raider fans erupted on to the field. Andy Mayer signaled with his hand across his neck that our throats were cut, it was over. Newt Nixon took his shirt off to the delight of the crowd and started whirling it in circles above his head. When his teammates approached him he ran away from them forcing them to chase him toward the corner. Coming toward them in the other direction was Christopher, who had also pulled off his shirt. As if Christopher and Nixon choreographed the moment, the two met in a leap and a chest butt that nearly knocked both of them off their feet when they landed.

Without anyone paying attention to us, Bobo called Luca over.

"Play on top. Don't give up. St. John would never give up."

Most teams would have been numb after that goal. But once the Crusaders watched Christopher make a spectacle of himself, it lit a fire inside each player. It didn't happen from anything we said. I know I never said anything. With Bobo standing beside me, outside of the few comments he made to Luca, I know he didn't say anything to the players either.

Two minutes later, Luca deked Danny, cut into the Crusader eighteen and was one on one with the keeper when he was pummeled from the side by Delaney. Luca buried the penalty shot low and to the right to make it a one goal difference. Billy Castil grabbed the ball out of the Raider goal and ran it to midfield.

The next six minutes were fast and furious. The ball continuously stayed on the Raider side as our back line and outside midfielders continually dumped the ball in or crossed it in front of the Raider goal. Each time we just missed a deflection or header goal the crowd "ooohed and aahhed."

Then the miracle happened. With time close to expiring on the center ref's watch, Adam Jackson placed a rushed corner kick into the six yard mixer. As all the boys collectively leapt into the air, somehow, Luca timed his jump and hit the ball as he was running toward it in the opposite direction, striking a bullet with his head into the far and open side of the net.

Now it was our time to revel. In the sheer pandemonium, Bobo and I hugged like a couple of fools before we were tackled by the players on the bench. As I lay on the ground, I looked up to make sure the center ref ran to midfield to signal the goal. Within seconds he blew his whistle to signify the game was over. Bobo and I had to calm down our team so we could listen to the center ref explain the rules for overtime. There was no golden goal he told us. There would be two ten-minute periods followed by a shoot-out if the game was still tied.

It may have not have mattered what the rules were for the overtime. The air was sucked out of the Raiders. They looked like a team that already lost. Luca scored four minutes into the first over time, giving us a one goal lead going into the second ten minute period. In the second overtime, with the Raiders pushing up Kelleher and Delaney, Luca was able to win a ball at midfield. He played a square pass over to Pepe, who had time to lob a ball over the top of Danny Livingston to Adam who sped toward the goal by himself. Danny, being the fastest player on the field, caught Adam, and forced him to slow down his dribble. Adam stutter-stepped the ball, giving himself just enough room to cross the ball toward Luca who was running at full speed toward the net. When the ball came across, Luca turned himself into a missile, flying through the air and nailing it past the Raider keeper.

It was over!

What a relief I thought, but then I saw Bobo sprint at full speed toward the Raider goal.

"Luca, Luca," he yelled. When I heard him call out Luca's name I followed, cutting through the clutter of people moving toward me like a kick-off return man in football. I knew the concern in Bobo's voice meant Luca was either hurt or ready to fight.

CHAPTER 13

WHEN I ARRIVED at the scene, Bobo was on the ground with his knees dug into the grass, holding Luca's head in the palms of his hands. Danny Livingston was standing above Bobo, crying, and pointing at Christopher who was behind the net.

"He told me to do it, he told me to do it!"

A crowd of people already stood between Christopher and me. When I looked at Luca I could see he was knocked out. Bobo and a tournament medic worked frantically at opening his mouth to make sure Luca didn't swallow his tongue. It's all I could stand to watch.

I looked at Danny. "What did you do?"

Danny didn't have time to answer. Dan Stemkowski, the state cup tournament director, saw the whole thing happen.

"You're suspended son, you won't play another

minute this year," he said to Danny. That's was also the moment I heard Bobo say,

"He's comin around Mario, he's comin around."

When I looked down I could see Luca's eyes barely open. Jenny appeared next to Bobo and helped lift Luca up so he could rest his head against her lap. Sensing something was about to happen, like a couple of security guards, Hopper and Andy Mayer put their bodies in between me and Christopher.

"He's not worth it Mario," Hopper whispered to me.

I couldn't help myself. The burning sensation I knew so well returned in full force. I pushed the two of them away and made a mad dash toward Christopher, who was standing with his arms crossed—smirking. As I tried to clear out a path of humanity in between Christopher and myself, the tournament officials along with team staff and dads got in my way.

"I'LL KILL YOU," I shouted. "I'LL KILL YOU—YOU LITTLE MOTHER FUCKER!"

As I reached for him, Christopher stood motionless; calmly chewing his gum with a look only a psychopath could have—like a punk at the zoo egging on a caged lion, he was at ease, at ease with the distance of safety the wall of men in front of me provided him.

"Your nightmares are just beginning," he said to me with a devilish grin, while I grasped through the crowd to get to him.

Men were holding my arms and legs. I had so many

faces around me I felt like I was in a rugby scrimmage. I wrestled with men I never met before. Sweat poured from my face to my chin and I could taste blood in my mouth from biting my tongue.

Finally, I had no more strength left. I caved to the demands of the men and let them push me back ten yards or so. Almost stumbling over Bobo, who was still kneeling on the ground, I heard him say softly as I caught my balance. "How could a man with Christ in his name be so cruel?"

As we sat at a picnic table near the tent where the awards ceremony was going to be, Jenny and I were briefed by Dan Stemkowski on what he had witnessed, what exactly had transpired?

According to Dan, after Luca slid and scored the final goal, his momentum placed him close to the goal post where the ball entered the net. When Luca stood up to celebrate he didn't see Danny Livingston sneaking up. Danny threw a ferocious elbow to Luca's head, smashing it against the goal post. That accounted for the two welts on each side of Luca's head.

The medic supervisor told us to take Luca to the ER to check for a concussion.

"He looks fine now but you can never be sure with injuries to the head. You must be cautious," he told Jenny and me. Jenny closed her eyes and put her hand on her stomach like she was in pain.

"Are you OK?" I asked her.

"The baby is kicking. She's pissed off."

"Did you say she's pissed?" I responded. "Is that wishful thinking?"

"Oh, it's a she alright. And nobody messes with her brother."

"Andy Mayer came over the table to apologize. His shirt was ripped and you could see a few finger swipes on his arm where I'd grabbed him during the wrestling match already beginning to bruise. He had a white towel in his hand that he used to wipe perspiration beads from the top of his head.

"You're as strong as a bull," he told me, running the towel over the top of his silver hair. "I don't blame you one bit for what you did. If somebody tried to hurt my kid I'd have done the same thing."

Bobo came over and put out his hand for Andy to shake.

"How you doin old man," Mayer said to Bobo.

"It's time for the kids to get their medals," replied Bobo.

Jeff Hopper presented the trophies to the boys at the tent. In his speech, he spoke of the game as the greatest comeback in the history of state cup. It was also the first state cup championship the Rochester Crusader club had ever won. Based on his performance during the entire tournament, Luca was awarded the MVP medal. Since he was holding an ice-pack to one side of his head while he sat at a table, Hopper came over and placed the medal around Luca's neck. The parents, players and remaining tournament staff members gave Luca a round of applause. Luca waved casually to all of them to let them know he appreciated the hand they gave him.

On his own initiative, Luca put his ice pack down and gingerly stood up on his feet. It became very quiet as Luca pulled the medal over his head with his right hand.

"This medal belongs to Bobo," he told the crowd. "He's the MVP. He's the one who got us here."

Jenny couldn't help but cry as the crowd cheered again. Luca calmly walked over to Bobo who sat inconspicuously at the corner of the table. When Luca held the medal over Bobo and fitted it around Bobo's head, a roar went up among the team.

"MVP! MVP!MVP!" chanted the Crusader players and parents.

In his humble way, Bobo motioned to the boys that their chants were too much. He nodded in acknowledgement to the entire group and quietly slipped away.

Mothers from both teams flocked around Jenny to make sure she was feeling alright with the baby. For about ten minutes or so, prior to us packing up and heading south down the freeway, Jenny received more attention than Luca.

Everyone we spoke to was conciliatory. Andy

Mayer assured Stemkowski that Christopher was fired and wouldn't work again in the Raider soccer club. Stemkowksi assured us Sonny Christopher would never coach or train another team in the state of Michigan. While they were talking, Fred Castil brought a blanket to our truck to wrap around Luca up in for the drive home. Hopper slung Luca's bag over his shoulder and stuffed it in the bed of my truck. Bobo was like a grandmother, doting on Luca and Jenny in the back seat, making sure the two of them were comfortable with the blanket and pillows stuffed to their sides.

He kissed Luca softly on the top of his head. "I will say good prayers for you on the way home."

Through a half opened window, we said our good-byes to everybody. Like the first time I drove Luca home from the hospital after he was born, I cautiously looped turns and rolled the truck to stops in order to protect him and smooth out the ride. Through the rearview mirror, I watched Jenny and Luca settle in. Luca's head rested on Jenny's shoulder with the ice pack wedged between their two necks.

"Are we going to the hospital," Luca asked as I passed a Burger King and Arby's.

"We're headed that way now."

"Which one?"

"The one you were born in, Troy Beaumont."

"I was born there?"

"Thirteen years ago."

Jenny gave me a look I saw in the mirror.

"Be quiet the two of you," she said to both of us. "Luca you need to rest."

"I'm fine mom."

"No you're not. You have two large bumps on the sides of your head and you might have a concussion. You must be in all kinds of pain."

"Not really."

"Luca. Daddy and I are worried about you. You must have been scared being knocked out like that."

"Not really."

"Are you sure? I know I would have been."

"It's weird mom. I don't remember anything after I scored. I just remember I had the most beautiful dream."

When I heard Luca mention that he had a dream I peeked into my mirror at the two of them. Turning slowly on to the I-75 entrance ramp, a tenseness boiled inside my stomach as I thought about the possibility Luca was becoming delirious.

"What was your dream about?" Jenny asked innocently.

"It was awesome mother. It simply was the most beautiful place. I was in a beautiful room, a room of white walls, like the tile in grandpa's basement—so shiny and cool to the touch. Dad's sister Sofie was sitting on a couch next to me holding a baby."

Oh no I thought. I felt my throat tighten up. Luca continued.

"I saw a lot of people from the pictures in grandma's room. They were so nice to me. Dad's sister was telling me jokes but I can't remember them and then Bobo showed up with a medal and put it around my head three times. Every time he put the medal around my head he called me St. John... St. John of the Midfield. I felt so good I didn't want to leave."

After Luca spoke of the dream, I lost it. Emotionally, I was ready to break down so I turned off the freeway to a gas station that sat alone off the exit next to a truck stop and a diner.

"What's wrong honey," Jenny asked. "We just got on the freeway."

"I forgot to go—I gotta go badly."

I parked the truck, making sure Jenny couldn't see my face. I stood in line behind people waiting to pay at the register, holding back my tears before I asked for the key to the restroom.

When I opened the door, spider webs stretched like feathery yarn from the top of the door, while the stuffy smell of standing urine and excrement assaulted my nostrils, making me think twice about entering. What the hell I am doing here, I thought to myself, holding my breath.

I locked the door. Then the emotional dams broke and it all poured out. I cried, I cried hard, like when my mother had to leave to go to Glen Eden, or when my sister Sofie drowned the day the car she was a passenger in veered off the road and plunged deep into the West River.

I ripped the cross off the chain I wore around my neck and held it in the palm of my hand.

There, in the dimly lit restroom, in front of the urinal with rusty drip stains marking the porcelain, there in the stifling rancid odor of a rest stop bathroom, there, beneath the webs and dust particles circling like viruses in the hot confined air, I knelt on one knee and gave my confession.

"Please Oh Lord, make me a better man. Don't let me try to hurt anybody ever again. Let me prove to you that I can be an instrument of good, that I will break the chain of hatred and violence my family is known for, that I will sacrifice for your sake and your will so my children might be saved from pain and injury."

I heard an impatient knock on the door so I wiped my eyes on my sleeve and left the restroom. When I walked out and breathed in the natural chilled air, though my eyes watered, I immediately felt good again. A peace settled over me. I was revived and ready to see Luca and Jenny, revived and ready for the long trip to the hospital. Once in the truck, I looked in the rearview mirror and caught Jenny's expression of concern silently asking me if I was all right.

I nodded yes. Then I turned and gave both Jenny and Luca a firm look and a firm command. "Whatever you do—Don't for the life of you let Grandpa know anything about this."

Thinking of what I had just confessed it was my hope the matter between Christopher and me could come to a peaceful resolution. I wasn't ready for Frankie to impose his brand of swift and fatal justice.

CHAPTER 14

I N THE AFTERMATH of the state cup game, the rest of my fall was spent in one hearing room after another, between league, state, and national boards. Luca's medical exam determined that he had received a grade three concussion. It was my feeling, and my lawyer, Marcello Bommarito concurred, that these organizations were being very helpful in order to avoid a damaging lawsuit.

At one hearing, Danny Livingston and his father, pleaded for leniency. Living up to my promise with God, I spoke on Danny's behalf, expressing my opinion that Danny was pressured or duped into trying to hurt Luca by Sonny Christopher. Danny explained that Christopher had practiced with him in the preceding weeks leading to the cup match on how to throw an elbow. It was a move that was intended only for one player—Luca Santini. Danny went on to say that after the games first overtime, he received the signal from

Christopher from the stands, a signal where Christopher held two index fingers and pointed to his own eyes. I told the panel of three I had forgiven Danny and was hopeful he could resume playing again, in the club of his choice. Afterward, Danny and his father hugged me and personally apologized.

Though Luca could go to school, when it came to playing soccer, he had to take a couple of months off. He continuously had migraines that forced him into his room where he could close the shades and curtains, keeping any light from coming in. He kept an ice-pack on the back of his head for hours until the pain subsided. Sometimes the pain was so severe he would vomit, which often made him feel better and signaled the migraine would soon be over.

The doctors told Jenny and me that the headaches were normal in the recovery process of a patient who experiences a significant concussion. They also told us it was not uncommon for the patient to have blurred vision, some memory loss, and incoherent thoughts. When Dr. Rasmussen discovered I had boxed in my young life, he was surprised I had never received a concussion.

"No," said Jenny. "Memory loss and incoherent thoughts are normal for Mario."

"Very funny," I responded to the banter. "Pregnant women can get away with that kind of talk."

Meanwhile, Christopher, who could no longer coach

or train for any team affiliated in the state, shacked up with Sally Livingston and forced her to work at a 7-11 in Fraser just so the two of them could survive. To complicate his life, his former girlfriend from Louisiana caught up to him and phoned Michigan soccer officials to tell them what Christopher had done to her. She even contacted a Macomb Daily writer who investigated Christopher further and wrote a major story chronicling Christopher's criminal past.

I was done with Christopher. I didn't want to see or hear of him again, let alone read about him. He was no longer able to work with soccer teams in the state of Michigan. He couldn't hurt another player again. The paper hit the trash can and I concentrated on work until Frankie walked in my office and dropped the Macomb Daily on my desk.

"Is this what your sport of soccer is all about?" he asked.

I acted like I'd never met Christopher before and refused to be goaded into a discussion.

"The fuckin' guy's an animal," said Frankie as he walked away.

* * *

In the early part of December, Luca resumed training with the team. In his fourth session back, as we practiced on the big field indoor at the Premier Training Center in

Macomb, Township, Pepe's mother Gloria approached me as I leaned over the drywall in the upstairs viewing area.

"Is Danny here? Is he coming back to the team?"

"I'm not aware of that. Why?"

"I thought I saw his mother Sally sitting in her car in the lot."

"Are you sure?

"I think it was her. Maybe I'm wrong."

Bobo and the boys were wearing their state cup championship t-shirts that Hopper surprised the boys with two days earlier. Bobo was gliding across the turf of the field, immersed as always into the scrimmage with the boys, becoming one of them as he assumed the part of the neutral player, capable of receiving passes from both teams.

"Puuurffeect, puuurfect," he stated over and over.

Whenever he wanted to send a crossing ball toward the net for a header he would announce a boy's name.

"Billy, Billy, special delivery coming," he would alert the player.

The boys lived for the Bobo scrimmage. It was the high-light of their day, to be side by side, next to the master, running, dribbling, passing, fighting for the ball—trying to imitate Bobo's movements as they played, until over time, as Jenny observed, they all became little Bobo's.

It didn't matter to Bobo who the boy was or what team the boy was on, or his age—Bobo didn't discriminate. If the boy had a ball and wanted to play, he was available. Even at tournaments, with teams we were about to play, Bobo would work on a move with a member of the other team just to help him out. Of course, that irked Fred and a few of our parents, but that was Bobo, he was for the game, the good of the game, and though he was our coach, he cared little about the scores. He cared about the players developing, about the players honoring the game, about the players chasing, what he called, "big dreams."

I was still upstairs, and noticed the door swing open to the field below. Fred and his wife stepped onto the turf looked around anxiously, and then looked up and spotted me.

"Come on down Mario. We've got problems," said Fred with a serious look.

When I made it over to where Fred and Marianne stood, Marianne handed me a bulletin like it was dirty, like somebody had sneezed on it.

"We found a bunch of these pinned to the wall in the entrance way," said Fred.

I started to read what was written on the official looking document. Immediately I thought of Sally Livingston and Sonny Christopher. The bulletin was written on what appeared to be official letterhead of the city of Fraser. Yet, I noticed right away that the writing was typed in an old font, and it was written by a supposed supervisor of security at a local store called Minors. The letter's content warned the public about a man named Bobo Stoikov who was caught at the store committing a possible sexual act while looking at little boys in the toy department.

As I read, without warning, Marianne shrieked, "Billy," so loudly it hurt my ears.

"What's wrong?" I asked her. "Practice still has another half-hour to go."

"I can't have my Billy around Bobo any longer. This is a very serious charge."

"But it could be a false charge."

"Not when it's on official letterhead of a city! We have to go."

Of course, before she left the training center, Marianne had to tell all the other mothers in the lobby about the flyer. One by one, the mothers slipped their heads out the doors to the field and called their sons in. With only about six players left, Bobo finally stopped and looked at me from across the field with his hands held out. I waved him over.

"What's wrong Mario?" Bobo asked.

I motioned for him to sit down on a bench against the wall on the first field. "I've got to show you something," I sighed.

Bobo stared at the piece of paper I handed him. It dawned on me as I noticed a sort of blank look on his face that he might not be able to read English or understand what I was showing him.

"I don't read very well, Mario," Bobo said. "I need my glasses. It all looks like chicken scratch to me."

After taking a deep breath, I read what was written on the bulletin. Bobo didn't hesitate shaking his head.

"Ten years ago, I go to Minors in between indoor games during the Christmas tournament. They are right across the street from Total Soccer in Fraser." Bobo lifted his right hand and pointed his index finger to the sky. "I swear to God, Mario, all I do is walk around to kill time and look at some sporting equipment. A guard thought I might be trying to steal something so he took me in the back and questioned me. That was all that happened."

"You're positive?"

"Yes."

"Did the store call the police?"

"No police. I had nothing on me but a Styrofoam cup for my coffee."

All I could think of at the time was to send Bobo home for a couple of days until I could get the matter straightened out.

"Go home and relax," I told him. "Wait for my call. I think your buddy Sonny Christopher is behind this."

When Bobo walked away, his shoulders sagged, making my heart tug as I watched him leave the facility disheartened.

Alone on the bench, I thought of what he had asked me once, to not let them take away his team—the only thing he had. Other than his brother Jordan, who lived in Traverse City, 150 miles away, I was the only person he really spoke to, the only friend he counted on. Bobo lived a meager life, a life barely subsidized by the modest pay he received as a soccer coach. Sonny Christopher knew that, he knew Bobo was vulnerable to such heinous charges since Bobo could never afford to defend himself with the legal means necessary to fend off such serious allegations.

For whatever reason, my mind triggered an image of Bobo and his brother Jordan crossing through the Bulgarian mountain paths, clinging to each other and clinging to life. Then another image was triggered, an obscure moment I faintly remembered in my High School sixth hour American Literature class, a class I normally dozed off in. In one of my few moments of comprehension in Mrs. Tucker's class, I recalled her pointing out what the green light at the end of Daisy's dock meant to the Great Gatsby. It was a symbol of hope and promise for a new world, a place that transcended the socially-imposed limitations of Gatsby's life, a place where Gatsby or any ordinary fellow could dream of and rise to in a land called America.

Thinking of Bobo and his brother Jordan, I wondered if they too had those same dreams about America, as they cut their way through the steep, dense, and untamed woodlands of Bulgaria. Did they too see the green light ahead of them in the distance? Was it that green candle of hope that kept them from giving up, kept them from going back, kept them moving forward toward a new and better life, a life they heard was promised to everyone who came to America, a land of infinite opportunity and freedoms?

As I pondered Bobo's fate, I made a commitment to myself, that I would be Bobo's voice, that I would defend my friend's honor and reputation under any condition, against Christopher, against the Raiders, against the soccer community as a whole. I would take on anybody or any organization—at any cost.

That night, my ear actually swelled up from holding the phone for so long against it. There was a flurry of activity among the parents, league officials and the board members of the Rochester Crusader Club.

Hopper called and told me he received the same bulletin in the mail. He too believed it to be a fraud as he had recognized a few handwritten words on the letter to be slanted in a style of writing he remembered uniquely belonging to Christopher. Hopper went on to tell me that a couple of club's fathers were police officers in Shelby Township. He had asked the two men if they and some detectives could stop by our house over the next day or two to start an investigation. When he asked if I would meet with them, I immediately agreed.

Jenny's a fighter. She was upset and outraged by what she knew were false accusations. Early the next morning, she was on the phone with the Personnel Manager at the Minors store. After reviewing their files, the manager, insisted there wasn't anything available concerning an incident at their store involving a man by the name of Georgi "Bobo" Stoikov.

I drove down to the municipal offices of the city of Fraser, and showed the shift supervisor the document that was written on their letterhead.

"We would never send anything out like this," asserted Sergeant Maxson. He made a copy of the bulletin so he could start his own internal investigation. Another police officer, who overheard our conversation, recalled a person asking about a man named "Bobo" under the Freedom of Information Act.

"That's a name you don't hear every day," he explained to us.

At 2:30 pm, Jenny received a call from my mother letting her know my father and she were stopping by in an hour or so. Mom went shopping for the baby and wanted to drop off some items while Frankie wanted to see Luca.

By 3:35 pm, I received a phone call from Jeff Hopper again. This time, I could tell by his tone that the matter involving Bobo had become more serious.

"Mario," said Hopper. "The detectives and police officers should be there any minute."

"Not today," I said to Hopper. "You never told me they were coming today. My father and mother are coming over. I don't want this place crawling with cops."

Hopper acted like he didn't understand.

"Mario, this is much too serious now."

"What do you mean now?"

"I don't know how to say this to you. Please don't tell Jenny this… but… the word now on the street is that Bobo… And Luca… had a…

"Had a what?"

"An inappropriate… an inappropriate relationship."

I bit my fist until it literally bled. Stretching the phone cord to its limits, I moved across the office and quickly shut the door.

"What the fuck are you talking about?"

"Ten minutes ago, I received a phone call from that Macomb Daily writer that did the story on Christopher. A confidential source told him about Bobo possibly molesting Luca. Now he wants to write a second story."

"You've got to be fuckin kidding? Not only do I trust Bobo, those two have never been alone. I've been there with them every second they've been around each other!"

Jenny heard me yelling and tapped on the door. I held my hand to the phone as she said,

"Is everything ok?"

"Yes hon. I'll be right out."

"Mom and Dad are here."

"I got to go," I told Hopper as I quickly clicked down the receiver.

Knowing the police would be knocking on my door soon, I rushed out of the room and pulled my father aside. Both Jenny and my mother could tell by my behavior and the sweat on my brow that something was wrong.

"Honey, what's going on," asked my mother, who demanded a kiss before I could take Frankie by the hand down to the basement to talk.

Downstairs, my father didn't waste time or words with me, realizing something bad was happening. He pinned me against the wall with his two giant hands.

"Give it to me straight. What's going on?"

"There's going to be police here."

Frankies eyes widened, like I was ratting him out. "Police?"

"Not for you. It's about Luca."

Now he was really upset. The veins by his eyebrows bulged with blood and pulsated like two giant snakes breathing hard after digesting a big meal.

"Not that fuckin' asshole I read about in the paper?"

The doorbell rang. I looked at Frankie, then upstairs toward the door.

"Do me a favor. Stay calm and stay in the kitchen. Keep Mom away. I'll explain everything to you as soon as I get rid of them."

"You're going to tell me everything's all right," were Frankies lasts words to me as I climbed the steps two at a time back up to the kitchen.

Because Jenny recognized two of the police officers, Steve Jennison and Mark Hamil from the club, she felt at ease letting them into the house. Jennison and Hamil shook our hands, while two stern faced detectives flashed their badges to us before we invited them into our family room.

Sergeant Lupa, the lead detective, showed us the document to us and settled both our nerves by telling us he knew the letter was fraudulent.

"A first-year law student could figure that out," he said to everybody in the room. Then, without hesitation, with the other two officers still chuckling, detective Lupa glanced at both Jenny and me.

"We're here to speak to Luca. Is he home?"

Jenny, who was sitting on the edge of the sofa chair due to her size quickly asked,

"Luca? Why would you need to speak to Luca?"

"Don't get excited mam," said Sergent Lupa.

"I'll get any damn feeling I want," retorted Jenny back. "What the hell does this have to do with Luca?"

From the shadows of the kitchen, mother walked out, equally concerned, with an "I'm demanding an answer" look on her face as well. My father stayed back, hiding in the darkness.

"There are allegations of a man named Bobo molesting your son."

"What?" said Jenny, looking at me like I had secretly kept something away from her.

I put up my hands as if showing her I had nothing to hide. "This is new to me as well. This is a false accusation—a total fabrication by Sonny Christopher and Sally Livingston!"

Jenny suddenly grabbed her midsection and screamed in pain.

"Aaah, my God!" she shrieked, falling slightly backward. Every man in the room was on his feet in a split second.

"This is not a good time," my mother shouted. I rushed to the bathroom to get a cool wash cloth. Hearing his mother scream, Luca flew out of his bedroom to see what was happening.

"We apologize," said Sergeant Lupa, frantically picking up the documents from our coffee table that he had neatly stacked in rows. Jenny squealed again, louder this time to where my father had no choice but to push his head from inside the kitchen to see what was going on.

"We have to get her to the hospital," said my mother.

"We'll escort the two of you there right now," said Officer Hamil. Jenny started breathing heavily through the pain. In the confusion, as the police and detectives hurried to the door, I found Jenny's shoes and slipped them on her feet.

"You're a month early," I said to her, squeezing the shoes on.

"It could be nothing but false labor," she choked out.

"Help her up, help her up," my mother ordered, darting her head back and forth between Luca and me.

It was then, right then, as I struggled to raise Jenny from the sofa, that my father and I locked eyes. Still in the kitchen, still in the shadows, I saw the dark anger rise in Frankie's eyes. There was nothing to say between us. He understood my anger, knew where it resonated, felt it like I did simmering inside. He would enforce my justice on the guilty.

As clear as I've ever understood somebody, I knew what Frankie was about to do, and I knew, in my current situation, there wasn't time to stop him.

CHAPTER 15

THERE WAS NO place to hide at the hospital. Jenny's contractions continued and with her being worked up regarding the situation with Luca and Bobo, it was hard to make eye contact with her. I felt like she was throwing daggers at me every time we needed to speak to each other. The pain and hurt in her eyes were too much for me to bear.

Luca stayed home with Frankie. My mother was with us at the hospital, getting in the way of the doctors and nurses as they moved in and out of the small curtained room inside the emergency room.

More than an hour later, they moved Jenny to the maternity ward and put us in our private room. Jenny's obstetrician, Dr. Wingate, arrived within the hour.

Jenny's water had not broken. Though the contractions she experienced at the house were fairly severe, she had only minor contractions since entering the hospital. After examining and interviewing Jenny with me out of the room, it was Dr. Wingate's medical opinion that the premature labor pains were due to the considerable stress Jenny was under. When he spoke privately to me out in the waiting room, he told me Jenny wouldn't tell him what upset her so much. He stared at me waiting for an answer.

How could I answer him? Was I supposed to tell him that my son's soccer coach was accused of molesting my son and the rumor had spread throughout the entire soccer community? How do you share that kind of news with someone? Not knowing what to tell Dr. Wingate, I mentioned the problem was me. I expanded on that by saying I hadn't been very attentive lately, and I had been spending a lot of time at work Jenny was probably feeling alone and blah, blah, blah, blah... You get it—all the excuses I could think of to deflect his attention away from the truth, or what I considered, the family's business.

Dr. Wingate told me to prepare myself for the long haul that Jenny was not ready to be released and was being monitored. He was taking no chances with her condition and mood. "I've never seen her so down and upset, it's not healthy for her or the baby." he said to me before he stood up and left the room.

My mother offered to go home to get some personal items for Jenny. She returned almost immediately arm-in-arm with a priest. She introduced me to Father Harrington, her old parish priest from St. Sebastian's church. Father Harrington, a tall man with a thick head of gray hair was at the hospital to pass out Communion to the Catholic patients.

With a few hours since her last contraction, Jenny finally let me beyond her wall of defense, allowing me to hold her hand as she lay in bed.

"I want this baby so much," she told me repeatedly, gazing endlessly up at the ceiling.

It was a harrowing night. Sometime around 3a.m. the contractions started again, this time more intensely, that I swear I wanted to hide every time Jenny screamed. Her grunts echoed through the hallway—chilling the entire floor trying to sleep in a deep concentrated fear. There is nothing more difficult than to watch a person you love so much experience so much pain. All I could do is pray it would end soon and well. When my mom came back to the hospital to bring me a change of clothes, she also brought me a rosary. I clenched it closely as I sat in the room's chair, hiding my face every time Jenny's head would lift off the pillow to let out a gut wrenching shriek.

By 7 a.m. the contractions were over. Jenny hadn't even dilated to one. Under Dr. Wingate's orders, the nurses, continued to monitor her and treat her as if the baby would be born in the next couple of days. Neither Jenny nor I had slept all night. Once Jenny fell asleep, with my energy spent, I positioned myself in her room's chair and caught a few hours of sleep as well.

When I woke up, Jenny was still asleep so I headed downstairs to grab a snack at one of the vending machines. As I pulled my wallet out of my back pocket to see how many single dollar bills I had, a news flash came across the TV monitor on the local news channel. Not knowing what time it was, and being incredibly hungry, my eyes wandered back to my wallet. When the anchor announced that a gruesome discovery was made of two bodies, badly beaten, riddled with gunshots, hanging back-to-back on a scarecrow's post in a deserted corn field out in Romeo, I knew without further information who the victims were.

When my eyes returned to the monitor, the station was showing head shot photographs of Sonny Christopher and Sally Livingston. The news cut to a live reporter who stood outside the farm next to a TV truck. The news cut to a helicopter shot of the entire farm. The news media and police had taken the place over.

When I looked around the room, there were only three people still waiting. One man slept, another woman worked on a cross-word puzzle, and a young teenage girl sifted through the pages of a People magazine.

Standing there, I knew I may not have been anywhere near Sonny Christopher and Sally Livingston at the time of the murder, but I knew I was guilty of murder. I was conflicted, with part of me wanting to jump on the corner ropes to raise my hands and cheer, and the other part realizing how I had become exactly like my father, how I was responsible for the death's of two human beings, how I was complicit in the murders even though I wasn't present.

I didn't have change to make a phone call to Frankie so I exchanged a dollar for two quarters from a kid with a Mohawk haircut standing near the phones. When Frankie answered, the first words out of his mouth were,

"How are Jenny and the baby?"

"Better now."

"Is your mother there?"

"I think she's sleeping somewhere in the third-floor lounge."

"Luca's doing great. He's still sleeping."

"Dad."

"Yeah?"

"I just saw the news."

"Can't talk on the phone son—you know that...

After a pause of twenty seconds or so, Frankie spoke the most diabolical of words... "Two down and one to go."

CLICK!

One to go? One to go I thought. I realized he must be talking about Bobo. Getting more change from a nurse at a desk, I frantically called back but Frankie didn't or wouldn't answer the phone. When I tried to call Bobo and he didn't answer I panicked.

If I could have screamed, it would have a thousand decibels louder than the piercing shrills Jenny made during the night. Inside my mind, you could hear a crashing crescendo of NO! NO! NO! levitated from the depths of my soul.

I searched for my car keys in my pockets. I didn't have them. I must have left them upstairs next to the chair or on Jenny's food tray table.

I ran the stairs to the room, snatched the keys without waking Jenny, and then ran to the waiting room to my mother. I had to shake my mother several times before she opened her eyes.

"Is the baby born, is the baby born?" she asked.

"No, no, I have to go. Watch Jenny until I get back."

"Where are you going?"

"I'll be right back!"

I'd been to Bobo's apartment. Maybe I thought at the time, that I could beat the killers there. My tires squealed as I spun from my parking space. I passed two cars getting out of the parking lot, then turned on two wheels on to Dequindre Road and headed south toward 696.

If I could just get to the freeway, just get to the freeway, I thought, just a quick nine miles, a quick nine miles and I can beat them there, I can beat them there. I weaved myself in between car after car, going

70, through two lights that just turned red, past 18 Mile Road, past 17, past 16. If I keep making the lights I can do this I told myself, I can do this.

My mind—filled with static and scrambled scenes—abruptly unleashed a barrage of different thoughts and visual pictures in the panorama of my head, like I was hallucinating, or schizophrenic, for between 16 mile and 13 mile I don't remember the road at all, just thoughts, just visions, just images, images from my catechism book of Elijah rising high on his chariot into a sky of fire, and Joseph emerging from darkness out of the snake pit, and David singing Psalms near a tree with his Shepherd's staff leaning against a rock, and then, and then, I saw Luca with his medal around his neck, saw Jenny giving birth to our baby, saw my mother in a straight jacket on a bed in a room, saw my father and his brothers ruthlessly beating Christopher and Sally with baseball bats until their flesh... pulverized to a pulp—splitting and secreting muscle as mush... and their blood, squirting from deeply gouged wounds like spray from a gashed water-hose... and bone, splintering and shattering from thick fractures—bone marrow seeping from cracks as cartilage and nerve endings are ripped from swollen joints...

I'm going mad; I'm going mad I thought.

At 12 Mile Road I hit a red light and was suddenly aware of my surroundings. Stopped behind a landscaping truck in the left lane, I leaned over to see a slick black Tiburon in my side-view mirror. The horsepower in my Ford 150 was no match I thought, so when the light turned green, I let the Tiburon go first by me, and then I snuck behind him to the right so I could get to the upcoming freeway entrance ramp.

In a flash, in nothing more than a flash, the Tiburon quickly pulled into a corner gas station, while I, with my foot pressed down all the way on the accelerator swerved to my left around him and then pushed again hard on my accelerator, only to find as I blew by the right side of the landscaping truck to my surprise, that there was another truck, a much bigger truck that was stubbornly parked in the right hand lane, and unless I was a bulldozer, or a tank, the truck was going nowhere—for it had no intention of getting out of the way.

Like a dragon fly smacking your car windshield, like the way the last image vanishes from a clicked off TV, with no time to stop, and no where to turn, I hit the ice truck at 65 miles an hour, exploding my red pick-up truck like a cherry bomb and bringing my world as I knew it to nothing, nothing but blackness—to the most sudden of silences.

CHAPTER 16

I CAN'T RECALL THE exact time I stopped by St. Rene's on a Friday evening during Lent, though I can pin it down to the late eighties, when I had just returned from living in California. As I traveled down Ryan Road, it was the statue of Jesus in front of the Church that caught my attention, for it was close to two stories high and with the way the hands of Jesus were held out; it appeared to look in my mind, like Jesus was standing in line at a cafeteria waiting for somebody to put a tray in his arms.

I sat in the last pew, closed my eyes for a second and quietly prayed. A voice, a voice belonging I learned to a young priest named Father Doc, who, after kneeling in front of the first Station of the Cross, began singing exquisitely on his own, as a solitary tenor, in a way that his voice seemed it had descended from heaven, or could have easily belonged to any of the Saints and Martyrs, who there before the Christ, poured their heart and soul into their song—praying, praying in the most fervent of ways, that their greatest gift would rise and be pleasing to their Savior and Lord.

The dramatic moment gave me goose bumps. Today, when I rethink the moment I get goose bumps again just thinking of the purity and sincerity of Father Doc's song. Due to my accident, I'm a paraplegic, so I have tons of time on my hands to think of such things—not that I'm not active, but, when you look at my life compared to the way it used to be, I have the gift of time, the gift of thought, the gift of prayer—the ability to ponder all the experiences which have come about or touched me in my life.

My car accident allowed me a second chance. And yes, of course I would prefer to be able to move my legs but my arms are free and that's all that I need to hold my two year old little sweetheart girl named Sofie. I call her "baby cakes" and in my mind, there is no greater gift than to be holding her close so I can breathe in the fragrance of her skin. Of course, whenever she gets too close, like most babies, Sofie can't resist squeezing my rather large but typical Dago nose.

Can you believe Jenny was that strong? Can you believe that a woman, who while agonizing through the pain of child birth, already knowing her thirteen year old son will be ostracized by a community and would suffer greatly, and then, finding out her husband had just been involved in a terrible car accident and was fighting for his life somewhere in the same hospital where she was attempting to have a baby, could be so resolute as to will the child to life after experiencing the most excruciating pain for over two weeks? She's simply the bravest person I've ever known. Today, though I no longer can enjoy an intimate relationship with her, the two of us are closer than ever.

Mom didn't fare so well. She completely lost her mind after my accident and now is a permanent resident of Glen Eden on their fourth floor. Pa and I visit her often, sitting in the dark together; we pray a rosary next to her bed as she listens along, knowing we're there, and acknowledging us with little smiles and light touches of our hands as she dreams of her room in heaven and converses in a language of her own to her imaginary Polish friends.

Luca took a year off from soccer. With his idol's death and his father incapacitated, it was too much for a young teen-age boy to handle. He was traumatized, grief stricken to the point that he was diagnosed with clinical depression. I thank God my father was able to afford the best doctors who knew how to treat Luca in the early stages of his symptoms. In that first year after my accident, when I wasn't around at all, it was only Jenny and my father who could keep him from going astray. According to Jenny, Luca did get suspended from school twice for severely beating a couple of smart aleck boys who questioned his manhood. Evidently, once the other boys witnessed the results of those fights, they understood they better not bother him.

In the early years, when it was happening, Jenny didn't appreciate my father training Luca to fight. Today she credits Frankie's boxing lessons for allowing Luca to win his honor back. She also understands it was very important in the process of Luca making his comeback to the sport he loves.

Since his return to soccer, Luca has dedicated his career to Bobo. He's playing better than ever and just last week he was named to the regional olympic development team. His dream, or as he tells me, "the big dream he chases," is to someday make the national team so he can feed through-balls to Landon Donovan.

Frankie is still Frankie. Some things never change they say or as my Uncle Angelo would say, "It's hard to be good in a rotten world." As usual, Frankie was never a suspect in any of the murders, allowing him to continue to fly under the radar in all his underworld activities. He did suffer though. He lost his daughter twenty some years earlier and then he almost lost his son, the son he lived for and protected his entire life. Through the most desperate nights of my ordeal, though I couldn't see him, I felt his presence every night in my room while I clung to life in the hospital. What hurt him the most, what punished him more than any bullet in the head could is my refusal to speak to him for six months after I recovered. What he had done to Bobo in my mind was unforgivable—but I did make a pact with the Lord on becoming a better man, so over time, with some convincing from Father Harrington, I was able to keep my word.

Only Frankie, myself, and Father Harrington know who is responsible for the murders. As soon as I became conscious and could speak again, my first request was to give my confession. At my bedside, before I knew I was a father again, before I knew about Bobo's death, before I knew of my son's delicate condition, I confessed my sins, and the sins of the family to Father Harrington, after he pulled the see through dressing curtain between us in my IC unit. When I did confess, the weight of the world came off my shoulders, and my new life began, a life of goodness, of decency, of showing mercy toward my fellow man. I started to see the world in a whole new light.

And speaking of decency, even after Bobo's murder, the fall out from Sonny Christopher's whisper campaign that Bobo was a pedophile preying on my son and others was still rife in the soccer community. For that reason alone, many of the adults did not want to attend Bobo's funeral. From what I've been told, uproar from all the boys who played for Bobo left the parents with no choice but to attend. Peter Sentilli, Bobo's brother Jordan and the entire team from Bobo's first squad arranged the event, making sure everyone whoever played for Bobo was invited to the visitation, the funeral, and the wake.

Luca told me that at the funeral home, with the crowd spilling out on to the streets, the boys who played for Bobo wore a t-shirt with Bobo's picture on the front and his name on the back,. In a spontaneous celebration, the place erupted when the players started chanting, "BOBO, BOBO, BOBO!" Fred Castil, who was there only at his son Billy's insistence, uses the same last line every time he retells the story.

"I swear it was more raucous than a freakin rock concert."

Had I not had the accident, I could have saved Bobo. According to the newspaper accounts, and the police officers I spoke to, Bobo wasn't murdered until noon, around two hours after my car wreck. One officer I spoke to claimed the scene was so peaceful, with so little evidence, it was like Tinkerbelle committed the murder, slitting Bobo's throat and disappearing through thin air. The officer confided to me that he expected the typical horrifying look of a person murdered to be on Bobo's face, but instead, saw nothing but contentment and serenity revealed in his dying expression; as if he was satisfied with all he had accomplished in our world or like that of a man dreaming of a better place.

Bobo was sleeping in his massage chair, with the back reclined almost to the position of being flat. The cut across his throat was so thin they said, it was like a chef taking a hot serrated steak knife and slicing gently into Valveeta cheese. Though there were no fingerprints on it, the only evidence they had, or the only thing they saw disturbed inside Bobo's apartment was a magnetic plastic crucifix, which normally sat high above and behind the massage chair on the top of a metal filing cabinet. According to Sergeant Lupa, it looked to him like the killer was so bothered by the cross being above Bobo's head, he moved it to the window sill just prior to slitting Bobo's throat.

Today I keep the plastic crucifix with me at all times. It says, "Made in China" on the back of it, just above the magnet, and the plastic characters to the side of Christ are barely recognizable. Still I don't go any where without it. Be it work, be it a trip to a restaurant or one of Luca's soccer games, the Bobo crucifix always goes with me. When I touch the crucifix in my pocket, or hold it in my hand, it makes me think of Bobo the way I want to remember him—there in the open field, with the boys of summer standing in the tall grass holding their soccer balls at the top of the hills, running through the green pastures, down toward the meadow, to train with St. John... to be with St. John of the Midfield, — making the right runs, playing the perfect ball, striking the shot that finishes the attack—and Bobo smiling at everybody, waving at everybody, welcoming them in, to work, to train, to play, as he would say, "for 50 million."

WHITE FANG

WHAT WERE TWO teenage boys supposed to do? We had been working for six hours with our father, struggling to panel the dining room walls. We needed a little comic relief.

It was a simmering hot July day. There were baseball games to be played, girlfriends to go swimming with, and ice-cream sundaes waiting at Sanders over at the Macomb Mall. Instead of enjoying our summer day, we were stranded in our small suburban house with our dad, sweating in a room smaller than some people's closets. Three fans made a futile attempt to keep us cool as we walked in and out of the room to measure and cut the sheets of thin wood.

My father was bent over, taking a measurement for the next piece of paneling. His hair and clothes were peppered with sawdust and mixed with sweat that ran down the back of his white T-shirt. His pants were riding low, revealing the crack of his ass. It had been staring at my brother Mark and me for hours. To a teenage boy, the sight of your dad's ass is hysterical. Only a half hour earlier, my mother came into the room to check out our work and told my father to lift up his pants.

"Nobody wants to look at your hairy ass," she said to him.

"Shaa – dup woman", he replied. My father always had a difficult time pronouncing the word shut-up. But no one in the family had any difficulty in understanding what it meant—whether or not we heeded his command was a different issue.

Mark's job was to hold the paneling against the wall while our father sized and squared up the wooden sheet. I was the official gopher, the guy who brought the tool my father demanded. This meant I was smack dab behind him, about a foot or to the right of his sweaty two-inch ass crack.

While holding the paneling, my brother Mark looked over his shoulders and gestured to me with his head. For some reason, in that moment, I became real bold or real stupid—or both, which is not unusual for a teen-aged boy. I proceeded to hold a small thin paneling nail right above the crevice of my father's butt. Mark watched in disbelief as I dropped the nail and burst out with a loud laugh. *My father didn't even feel it*. Mark's shift in attention from the paneling he was holding caused the paneling to shift to the right just before my father pounded a nail. Oh boy. That was that. We waited for the explosion.

Dad was not calm, soothing, "we can work this out" kind of dad of the TV sitcoms. When he was upset, he didn't try to initiate dialogue, didn't try to come to an understanding, and didn't try to instill a life lesson in any type of conversation he might have with you.

No, he just came out swinging. It seemed, even before the bottom of the paneling fell to the floor, that my father had delivered three to four haymakers right over Mark's head, causing the dining room chandelier to sway.

"You son of a bitchin clown," my father shouted at Mark, charging Mark like a heavy weight fighter trying to cut off the ring. Mark kept backing up, still laughing, holding his arms across his face, until he tripped over my father's foot rest and landed between the couch and the coffee table. Mark put his legs up to protect himself from my father's hammering blows.

"Why is it every time I ask you to do some fuckin work you start clowning around?"

Mark didn't answer. He was just trying to survive.

"Tell me why, why, WHY!" my father shouted louder.

My mother, who was working with her flower pots, finally heard my father yelling and came storming into the room. She wedged her small body in between my father and Mark.

"That's enough, that's enough," she told both of them, as she pushed against my father's beer belly to back up.

"He's a fuckin clown," my father repeated, shuffling backwards as he stared Mark down.

* * *

That night, from his upper bunk, Mark told me he was going to get even with me.

"Trust me," he said. "You got a good one coming."

I decided to get Mark laughing again, to take his mind off avenging the incident.

"Pa never even felt that nail. It's probably still stuck inside his crack."

I heard Mark start to cackle above me.

"Marky—he's got a four laner there."

"What are you talking about?"

"Pa's got a four lane highway you can drive right down his crack."

Mark started to lose it again. My father heard us laughing and started pounding his fist to the wall from inside his bedroom.

Mark said, "Shhh—asshole." I just ignored him.

"He's got a four—bee Marky Magoo. That's a four laner to the darkest hell hole in the world. I saw tractor trailers running loads down there"

Mark started smacking his mattress above me in an

attempt not to laugh or at least not to be heard. Then, from the corner of my eye, I saw in the darkness, his light blue pillow being swung at me.

"Cut it out," he pleaded with me.

"What if the nail falls out in the bed and pokes him in his big fat ass?"

"Cut it out," Mark pleaded again.

"What if he finds it ten years from now and has to have it surgically removed?"

By now, Mark was howling with laughter. That's when the door opened. Thank goodness it was our mother.

"Do you want me to send your father in here?" she asked. The light from the hallway was so bright it forced me to squint.

"Shut the door, you're blinding us, Mark said to her.

"No mother," I quietly said, trying to play the angelic son.

"Mark just won't stop laughing."

"Haven't you gotten into enough trouble today son?" she asked Mark.

"Yeah-yeah, yeah," he mumbled. "Shut the door."

"Then quit talking and make sure you say your prayers."

When she closed the door, I whispered to Mark,

"How come we can't tell them to quiet down when he's bangin her head into the wall?"

"Shut the fuck up," he said to me. Then he repeated

what he told me when we first got into bed. "Remember. Revenge is all mine."

Who would know it would happen so suddenly. Mark usually took his time to retaliate, typically two to three weeks later. In this case, it was the very next day. He chose Church of all places, when of course, I was the most vulnerable. My mother and father could never get up early enough for the 8:30 am service. But as Altar boys at St. Athanasius, Mark and I were scheduled for the earliest Sunday Mass. On this day, the priest was Father Krieg, the toughest, crabbiest, old-school parish priest known to Catholicism. In fairness to him, on his good days, the kids liked him since he would play ball with us at recess, help us fly a kite in the church lot during the Parish picnic, or let us throw soft balls at him during his turn on the dunk tank at the annual church fair.

But if you forgot to genuflect prior to getting into your pew, talked or chewed gum during Mass, or got out of line in the hallways of St. Athanasius prior to the sound of the bell, he was the last person you wanted looking directly into your eyes.

My brother was slick. He waited for the Gospel reading, the perfect moment to enact his revenge. During the reading, the two altar boys face one another, on either side of the pulpit, while the priest reads from the good book. We were trained to stand as still as possible, like soldiers of the Lord, holding the Pascal candles while we looked directly into each other's eyes.

All his life, Mark was prone to nervous tics or compulsive face twitches. When Mark was younger, he would throw his chin up and his head back like a turkey, showcasing his long and skinny neck. He could be in on stage for the class play, at the plate in a pee-wee baseball game, or on the diving board at Somerset swimming pool, when suddenly he would lift his head back.

Later, he developed a weird tic, a grotesque contortion of his face that would last for a second then go away. My father called it his "sneeze-face," for it looked like Mark inhaled a handful of pepper into his nose.

Entering his teens, Mark came up with a new facial contraction, one that turned him into a neighborhood legend. It was aptly named, "White Fang." Somehow, don't ask me how, he started this weird thing where he began curling up his right lip, freezing it above his gum line, allowing his right eye-tooth, his fang, to reveal itself totally outside his lower lip. The few times I saw him do it, he looked like a snarling rabid dog.

During the beginning of the Gospel reading, I didn't catch a glimpse of him doing it right away. At first, I looked over him, above Mark's shoulders at the side pews, at some of the parishioners in the front row. I could see Mr. Keenan, the Council President and the biggest brown-noser in the Church, right up in the front row with his wife and six kids. Behind him, sat the supervisor of all Altar Servers, the only guy I knew who scared me as much as Father Kreig and my own dad.

Mr. Becignool was at odds with the culture of the early seventies. He expected "his" altar boys to keep their hair short and cropped tightly; and he forbid us to wear bell-bottomed pants like a "ninny"—his favorite expression. During our meetings with him, the first forty-five minutes were devoted to his ranting and raving about we were all ninnies, a bunch of no good hippie-loving pot-smoking suburban sissy boys.

Looking beyond Mr. Becignool and adjacent to his right shoulder, was Sandy Diotto, the hottest, most curvaceous girl in the eighth grade. It looked like her parents were standing next to her. The problem was, I couldn't see her body because Mr. Becignool was in the way. All that was available for me to see was her neck and face.

Oh please Mr. B, I thought to myself, can you move just enough, maybe just a centimeter, so I can see the wonderful curves of Sandy's body? I'll admit I'm a ninny if you do so. I had spent hour after hour in Miss Babbie's math class, staring at Sandy's breasts; savoring the moment she looked right back at me and smiled.

In the process of trying to get a better glimpse of Sandy Diotto, I imperceptibly cranked my head to the right at the slightest degree. Unfortunately, that's when

Mark's face came into view and I picked up, in full resolution, the infamous White fang, a solitary object, radiant against Mark's reddish pink lips, with an edge so sharp Count Dracula would be envious.

I tried not to laugh. I really did. I mustered up all my inner resolve, quickly recited prayer after prayer, bit my lip until my teeth penetrated through the tissue and secreted blood from the corners of my mouth— but to no avail.

The image of the White Fang was imprinted in my mind. The fact that Mark pulled this face off less than a foot away from Father Kreig and in front of a congregation of six hundred people pushed me beyond the limits of self control. My knees shook, the candle in my hand began to sway, I tried to look away from the fang, I tried, I tried, but with my resolve weakened, I could no longer restrain myself. Right there, in the middle of the Church service, five feet away from the holy altar, twenty feet away from the Supervisor of all Altar Boys, and two feet away from the Pastor of St. Athanasius for twenty-three years, I burst out in loud, uncontrollable laughter.

At first, I thought Father Kreig might swing the book at me and smack me in the face. Instead, he took the candle from my hands, grabbed my ear with one hand and jogged me past the sanctuary like a dog at a show, pulled me through the vestibule, and then in a crazed ten yard sprint, tossed me like a drunk gets thrown out of a bar, right into the open vestment closet. My face caught on the longer garments, snapping their hangers off the rod, launching them across the small room. As if it was choreographed, Mr. B came through the parish hall entrance and along with Father Kreig, whacked me in a synchronized kick to my rear end. The two of them proceeded to kick and smack me until I assumed they got tired.

"How dare you do such a thing in such a holy place," Father Kreig exploded.

"Father, he's nothing but a fuckin ninny," chimed in Mr. B.

"I want his parents in here before he can go to school next week."

"I'll take care of it Father."

My head was jammed against the molding in the closet. Three or four robes were wrapped around my body and head. Breathing deeply, I listened to both Father Kreig and Mr. B, while praying they would leave.

When they finally left, I pulled myself up to a sitting position in the closet. It was then, in the tight entrance way of the sacristy, that I saw Mark, coming to get the unblessed hosts, holding his hands in prayer with the pious look of a Saint on his face. He didn't turn to me and he didn't smile. Retaining his holy expression in preparation for his return trip to the altar, Mark halted only for a second, just enough time to flash "White Fang" at me again—letting me know he was a force not to be reckoned with, and letting me know, he had just received the sweetest revenge a guy could ever ask for.

MY DOG TIM

MY PARENTS BROUGHT home a short-haired collie mutt two months before I was born. My four-year old brother, Glenn, named the dog after a boy he had played with only one time in a sand box. Tim's family had suddenly moved when his father was sent to Viet Nam in the early 60's. Perhaps my parents thought a dog would make up for the loss of Glenn's new found friend.

By the time I was four, Tim was close to 75 pounds and just a bit over three-feet high. We could look each other in the eye if Tim lowered his head and I stood on my tiptoes. As a young boy, Tim saved me from a thousand monsters. Frankenstein, Dracula, and the ever-present werewolves, stealthily slunk out of sight when Tim was close by, keeping a safe distance between them and me. Of course I knew they were looking for an opportunity to return. Deathly afraid of Tim, these monsters patiently waited for my midnight dashes across the hallway to go to the bathroom. They delighted in the moments when my mother would send me on a mission to retrieve a canned good from our dark and damp basement—which clearly was Count Dracula's castle. There was an oddly sweet feeling in racing Tim up the dungeon stairs and leaving behind the moans and cries of the furnace, which surely were Dracula's victims. Moving away from the darkness, I knew I was closer to reaching safety. At the top of the stairs Tim always looked at me like he wanted to say, what the heck are you worried about? That Dracula wimp can't touch us.

However, full sunlight in the kitchen did little to keep other horrors at bay. Tim's protection was called on again to save me from having to eat liver, the worst meal, in my mind, ever to be prepared in culinary history.

Tim and I had a pact. We didn't need to look at each other. As soon as those horrendous "liver smells" started whisking around the kitchen, Tim knew he would be eating real well and I knew I was sneaking to the refrigerator after my parents went to sleep.

There is absolutely no way to disguise the texture and taste of liver—not that this deterred my mother from trying. She prepared the liver as though it was breaded chipped steak, topping it with ammogghio, my favorite Sicilian tomato sauce. Even this did little to improve the taste. I'd play along, thinking to myself, sure mother, sure, I can't tell the difference in texture between an organ and a piece of steak! You're fooling the heck out of me. Then I'd wait for her to turn back toward the stove, or for one of my brothers to spill his lemon-lime Kool-Aid, or for my father to begin his long dissertation on how the Japanese were invading America to take all of the automotive jobs away. All I needed was a little diversion to swipe the liver from my dish, put it in my napkin and place it beneath the table on my leg, where it would never be seen again.

What a pro Tim was! Despite his size, he found a spot to lay in wait under the table during dinner—without drawing my parent's attention to our grand scheme. When I carefully slipped the liver out of my napkin, Tim delicately removed the organ with the gentlest grip his mouth allowed.

Now normally, he chewed food nosier than a construction worker chomping down a twelve inch meatball sub. In these covert instances, complicit in our crime, he was as silent as a boa constrictor, as if he suffocated the liver and ingested it by unleashing his jaw around the organ—swallowing it whole. Above the table, no one could hear a sound as Tim savagely and silently, ripped, tore, and devoured the meat. I rubbed his back with my feet, letting him know he did a good job, letting him know he was the best friend a little kid could have.

At other times, Tim was less patient. As I played touch football with my brothers Mark, Glenn, Tom, and our neighborhood friends, Larry Bruscha, Johnny Krebbs, and Billy Coleman, my father and Tim watched from the living room window. Tim went crazy as we ran, tackled, and fell to the ground. Finally, my father would place a rolled-up paper in Tim's mouth, open the front door and let Tim shoot out in his mad run for a touchdown.

Tim was impossible to tackle; he was Gale Sayers, Walter Payton, and Barry Sanders all in one 75-ound bolt of lightning. He would change his speed, juke his head, and pirouette in the middle of a run. Just as you thought you had him he was gone. All we tackled was air! The game of chasing Tim would always ended with him sitting in our driveway, viewing all of his victims, sprawled breathlessly across the lawn on their bellies. Victoriously, Tim would drop the soggy paper from his mouth, letting you know the game was officially over.

* * *

When I was twelve, at the insistence of my Grandma Clare and mother, Tim became my assistant for one fateful day on my Detroit Free Press morning paper route. Though my father was against it, I can still see my mother and grandma standing in the kitchen in their robes and hair curlers, wagging their fingers at my father. My mother gave my father the sternest look.

"If not Tim, then you go," she shouted, scurrying out of the room with my grandma at her side. Pops just shook his head and looked at me.

"Don't ever marry a Pollock," he said to me, pointing at me as if he was giving an order.

Pops was working the early shift over at the bolt factory. He knew he couldn't take me. My brothers couldn't help; they had routes of their own. Tim was the only answer.

The edict not to let me go alone was based on a few incidents which had occurred the previous week. First, I was egged by some teenage punks making their rounds before school as they drove through the suburban streets. Then, as I was pedaling my bike home on Slumber Lane after finishing my route, another group of local derelicts maneuvered close to me with their car and pushed an iron rod in between my back spokes. My red Schwinn flipped on top of me as I skidded across the pavement, bleeding as the skin peeled from my legs and arms. As the car sped away, all I heard were the boys snicker, as I peered into the dark morning sky.

The third incident, which terrified me the most, was Bongo, the little black terrier mixed mutt of my best tipping customer—Mr. Toranado. In an attempt to bite me, Bongo crashed right through the middle window of their storm door. The dog was a maniac, a paperboy's nightmare. Every time I approached the house, the dog went berserk, running through the house, jumping at the walls, picture window and door. Three or four other times Bongo attacked me. Unable to control Bongo, Mr. Toranado must have felt badly about the situation. (Perhaps that's why he tipped me so well) I learned to defend myself by swinging a rolled up newspaper at Bongo until he left me alone.

With Tim running security, we left around 6:00 am. It was a warm spring day, with a thick and, to my overactive imagination, eerie fog settling in. Tim and I cut through the fog from street to street, with Tim patrolling the area around my bike while I stepped up to my customer's house to drop their Free Press paper in between the doors.

Everything was going well until we made it half-way down Rainbow Street, two doors away from Mr. Toranado. His light was on as Mr. Toranado was one of the few customers who waited for his paper in the morning. He told me once he couldn't take a dump until he drank a cup of coffee and read the front page of the Free Press.

Mr. Toranado must have opened his door looking for me, when Bongo, the slyest of dogs, raced out the door to attack on his favorite target. I heard Mr. Toranado yell, "Bongo, Bongo get back here," but it was too late. In the thick fog I could not see Bongo, but I could hear his dog tag swinging against the chain around his neck. Forgetting for a second that Tim was there, I braced myself and quickly rolled the paper up that was in my hand.

Evidently, Bongo wasn't born with a great gift of scent like most dogs. If he had, he would have known I wasn't alone. Had Bongo realized a big hulk of a dog named Tim was guarding his best friend to the death, Bongo could have avoided a painful skirmish. Instead, he tore through the fog, appearing in front of me six to seven feet away from my bike. That's when, from my adolescent viewpoint, the scene suddenly switched into super slow motion and became a memorable cartoon.

Have you ever seen the eyes of a dog bulge out as if they've temporarily left their sockets? Have you ever seen a dog put on the brakes after running at top speed and skid across a sidewalk like Wiley Coyote so quickly it burns the fur right off it's back end? That's what I saw when Bongo saw Tim, right next to my bike, coiled up on his hind legs, with the look of a murderer in his eyes, and the sharpest, whitest, longest fangs visible from an open mouth, salivating, ready to pounce on a small but sumptuous snack.

When the sound came back to my ears, Tim was closer to Bongo's tail than a NASCAR racer riding another driver's draft through a turn. They shot into the fog and from there it became a piercing trail of snarls, snips, screams, cries, and you name it until every lamp-light in the neighborhood flicked on and every neighbor in their robes ran across their lawns or the street to determine what was causing all the commotion.

When the blitzkrieg was over, an almost lifeless Bongo was curled in a heap, whimpering on the lawn. Mr. Toranado screamed at what I perceived as profanities at me in Italian. "I'll sue you and your dad for everything you have," he finally proclaimed in English, waggling his finger in the air as I looked up into the canyon like nostrils of his Italian nose.

First, the police came. Then, Mr. Rashke, my Free Press route supervisor came. He put his arm around me as I lifted the kick stand to my bike and told me to get Tim home. He would finish the dozen or so deliveries left on my route.

I was too nervous to ride my bike. My heart was racing. With Tim keeping pace, I ran next to my bike—two fugitives escaping the scene of the crime. We ran by the cemetery, the school, the big statue of Jesus standing erect, holding his arms out in the darkness at the roadside in front of St. Athanasius.

That evening, when Mr. Rashke came to the house, I was fired at twelve from my paper route for violating rules I didn't know existed. "See, see," were my dads words to my mother and grandma when Mr. Rashke dropped the bombshell on us. Pops pounded his fist on the table. "I wish you two Pollocks would listen to me once in awhile, I knew that dog wasn't supposed to go," my father bellowed.

"At least the boy wasn't hurt," responded my grandma, as she put out her cigarette in the kitchen sink. I was still unnerved and didn't pull away from her when she hugged me and gave me a kiss on the cheek.

The moment Mr. Rashke walked out the front door the fireworks started. The morning's events were more than enough to set off my father's Sicilian temper. Pops crashed a plate to the kitchen floor, porcelain exploding like shrapnel from a grenade.

"Children, get to your rooms," grandma shouted. My mother picked up a plate and threw it down as well.

"Two can play that game," she fumed.

Now it was on. My brothers scattered to safety throughout the house. Grandma grabbed my sister Sharyl's hand and pulled us to her room.

"Get behind the bed," she cried to us. Tim followed right behind, the look of fear in his eyes, nervousness you only saw in him when my father was mad. Tim managed to get half his body under the bed.

My grandmother stood guard inside the bedroom, peeking through the crack of the opened door. Whenever she felt like putting her two cents in she would open the door and stand inside the hallway, one hand on her hip, trying to yell over my mother to make a point. "You hit her and I'll call the police," shouted grandma.

"I've never hit her in my life," Pops shouted back. My mother was trying to calm him down. "Come on honey, come on, relax, relax," she repeated.

"SHA-dup, you damn Pollock's all stick together," I heard Pops say.

"I didn't know I was marrying two of you," he added. The door opened and slammed, which usually meant Pops was going to the Park or a movie, just somewhere to cool off. We were in the clear until he came back.

On that night, he came back within the hour and bolted into the living room, shouting my mother's name and telling her to turn on the TV.

Still in our rooms, we all ran to the living room to see what had upset Pops. Moments later the television warmed up and Jac Legof and John Kelly from Channel 2 news told the story. The police had found the bodies of a little boy and girl over on Squirrel road in Oakland County, ten miles from our house. The reporters announced that the murders were linked to other recent murders and they feared a serial killer was on the loose, a serial killer they dubbed the "Oakland County killer".

Grandma made coffee. My mother snuggled next to my father on the couch and held my little sister Sharyl on their combined laps. My brothers and I had settled on the floor with Tim in the middle, as a head rest, while we listened to the broadcast.

"What's a serial killer?" I distinctly remember my little sister asking as she played with a curl of mother's hair near her forehead.

No one replied. I cannot recall another word being

spoken that night. A hush fell over the room, and the entire neighborhood, a quiet apprehension that lingered from that night going forward and it changed my parents forever.

The next day, not one of the boys in our family had a paper route any longer. Two weeks later, a for sale sign went up on our front lawn. Pops and mom were moving us thirty miles north, out to the country.

* * *

Sometimes life isn't fair. At seventeen, I was strong and confident. With Tim it was just the opposite. After seventeen years, two strokes, and a huge gain in weight, he lost the ability to properly move his hind legs. At that time in his life, he usually stayed to himself in the laundry room.

On the day of Mark's graduation party, Tim struggled to get up and stiffly dragged his enormous body to the back door. He put his nose in the corner of the door and pushed it a bit until my brother Glenn opened it. The two of us lifted Tim's back end up so we could move him from the porch down to the grass.

Perhaps it was the excitement of the party that brought Tim to the backyard. Perhaps Tim remembered all the voices in the crowd, the friends, the neighborhood boys and girls, my aunts and uncles and cousins who had pet him a million times.

The party stopped. Without anything being spoken, our friends, family, and relatives all gathered around Tim as if he was about to perform a trick. Tim just looked at them all, his mouth open, his tongue hanging out, saliva thicker than jelly oozing from the curve of his mouth.

My brother Glenn got an idea. He ran into the house and came back with a rolled up newspaper. When Tim saw it, he lifted his head in approval, then tried to inch forward but stumbled. "Steady old man," Pops spoke. My brother Mark and I grabbed him, put our arms around his over sized body, lifted him up and got him balanced again. Glenn then put the paper in Tim's mouth.

What a magical moment. It was like the old Tim was back. Sure his body looked like it was on steroids and sure he couldn't move anything but his neck and head more than an inch or two. But you could tell by the look in his eyes that in his mind he was flying around the backyard again, zipping in and out of tacklers, shattering record speeds, twisting and turning away from his many attackers. On impulse, Glenn feigned like he was tackling Tim by jumping over him. Mark did the same while I slid under Tim. It was bad acting, worse than the Three Stooges but the crowd approved and gave Tim and the three of us a standing ovation.

That's when Tim dropped the newspaper. Tim struggled but got his legs beneath him so he could sit. He stared at the crowd still clapping, looking at all of them like he was being inducted into the Hall of Fame.

In the glow of it all, it was like Tim was receiving his "lifetime achievement" award for being a dog, and there, amongst the royal family, the dignitaries, the paparazzi, and you name it, he was being applauded, not for anything special he did, but for doing his job as a good dog, a decent hard working blue collar dog. He barked at all the right times, stayed in the back yard when the gate was opened, and kept intruders from entering our home.

I pushed my face against a dried out patch of fur next to his ear, feeling the scrape, and hugged him. "You still got it boy, you still got it," I told him, close enough to catch a furnace blast of his hot stale breath.

A month and a half later, Tim passed away. On the day of his death, the entire family gathered in his sanctuary, the living room, not wanting to be alone. We shared stories about Tim until we were yawning from fighting the sleep.

Deep into the night, I slid with my pillow and blanket and positioned myself behind my father's chair, where the carpet was worn from being Tim's favorite place to sleep. I thought of an old video my parents had taken of each of us boys as toddlers riding Tim like he was a horse.

And then I thought of my Grandma Clare's death and how Tim had placed his head gently on my thigh while I sat on the floor in my room. It was hours before I fell asleep on that longest of nights. Now in the blackness of the living room, through the eyes of a young boy, I could see how Tim's eyes glowed with a greenish tinge like a space alien as I darted across the hallway to take that dreaded midnight trip to the bathroom.

He was the only dog I ever had. How was I to act in the aftermath of his death? Should I pray? Should I cry? Seventeen-year old boys don't cry over a dog I thought.

My thoughts emanated from my mind like black and white images flashing from a television set. While the soft cries of my baby sister spilled out beneath her blanket, I lay there, squeezed between the paneled wall and my father's easy chair, gripping my pillow tight, knowing loneliness would soon overwhelm me, and knowing my years of being innocent and carefree were now way, way behind me.

Made in the USA
Lexington, KY
27 June 2014